JOURNEY TO THE CENTRE OF THE YOUNIVERSE

by G. N. IDRAH

(DOUGLAS HARDING)

Published by The Shollond Trust

87B Cazenove Road

London N16 6BB

England

headexchange@gn.apc.org

www.headless.org

The Shollond Trust is a UK charity reg. no 1059551

Manuscript typed by Danielle Bol-de Greve

Setting of book by rangsgraphics.com

Cover design by Sam Blight, based on an original drawing by Douglas Harding

ISBN 978-1-908774-46-0

CONTENTS

Preface

Douglas Harding (1909–2007) worked out a modern map of our place in the universe, first presented in 1952 in his great book, *The Hierarchy of Heaven and Earth* (described by C.S. Lewis as "a work of the highest genius"). In this profoundly original work of cosmology Harding takes the reader on a tour through the layers of the universe, from galaxies to particles, to find at the centre of this onion-like structure… nothing at all. But this nothingness isn't a dead, empty nothingness. It is aware and it is full. It is the Reality behind all appearances. It is who you and I really are. Yet who has read this book? Hardly anyone.

One of Harding's gifts was the ability to communicate about deep and complex matters in clear, non-technical language. But in the early 1970s he went beyond words by developing his 'headless way' experiments. These are a breakthrough because they share the non-verbal experience of the Centre rather than simply conveying ideas about it. After inventing the experiments, Harding would sometimes say, "You don't need to read *The Hierarchy*. That was something I had to work out. All you need do is look where you are."

This is true. But in spite of Harding downplaying *The Hierarchy*, the ideas in that book cannot be dismissed as one man's personal vision of the structure and functioning of the universe. *The Hierarchy* describes the way the universe is, and is more accurate than the current scientific model because it includes the observer. And yet, Harding's view is practically unknown.

In the mid-1970s Harding produced his *Youniverse Explorer,* a model of the universe that is not only an elegant simplification of the ideas in *The Hierarchy* but is also strikingly beautiful. Standing about 14 inches tall, it showcases the layers of the universe and indicates how they fit together in one living structure. This model is as important as the model of the globe, or the model of the solar system. Yet who knows about it?

When Harding was developing his *Youniverse Explorer,* he experienced a short but intense crisis which later he referred to as his 'dark night of the soul'. Through this breakdown he came to feel more deeply the nothingness of his True Self. Afterwards Harding valued this experience enormously, seeing this 'dying to self' as a vital part of his spiritual development, a breakdown that led to a breakthrough.

Around the time of this crisis, Harding wrote *Journey To The Centre Of The Youniverse.* Another child of *The Hierarchy,* this story presents through yet another medium the structure of the universe and the spiritual transformation that is born from travelling through the layers to the Centre. It is an odyssey that reflects Harding's breakdown and breakthrough.

Harding had a liking for quirky book titles with more than one meaning—*Head Off Stress, Look For Yourself, To Be And Not To Be*—*that is the answer.* For *Journey To The Centre Of The Youniverse,* he used the pseudonym 'G.N. Idrah', which is 'Harding' spelled backwards. Whether he intended it or not, this reflects the fact that when you arrive at the Centre after a helter-skelter journey through the layers, you experience a turn-around, a conversion. It's not surprising then if you feel back-to-front, turned upside-down and inside-out.

This is a dramatic story, a wild dream, at times a nightmare, at times a hilarious and subversive satire. It involves a quest, a monster and a shape-shifting hero, strange characters and dangerous goings-on, and an end that is a beginning—the tightest corner of Hell opening out into the widest smile of Heaven, the darkest of nights turning into the early morning freshness of the world. Are you prepared to wrestle with the angel till dawn? Only those that go the whole way will find the Whole.

Every time I read *Journey To The Centre Of The Youniverse* I appreciate it more deeply. It celebrates a fabulously real vision of the universe.

Richard Lang

Chapter 1: How It Began

It was freezing harder than ever out there. And quite windless and silent—except for, could it be a distant, snow-muffled wolf-howl? As I closed the shutters tight I saw that the stars, amazingly twinkly and bright against the black sky, were sparking off a glitter in the snow all the way to the edge of the forest. I shivered and hurried back to the fireside and Douglas the cat. Arched back, hair on end, *he'd* heard that howling too.

Little David on the mantle shelf, with nothing on but a marble loincloth and a sling, looked as cold as the brass Buddha beside him. I bent down and put on another pine-log, drew up my armchair, and settled down to watch the flames.

And then, a knock on the door! On such a night, so many miles from the road!

But I *hadn't* imagined that knocking. There my visitor stood, a slight, upright figure, dark against that star-strewn blackness.

"Could I..." he was saying, "could I warm myself up at your fire?"

As he stepped in out of the cold I mumbled something about his having lost his way.

His reply was a laugh that could have meant anything. He came up to the fire and sat down in the other armchair. Douglas, my tail-less Manx, at once jumped onto his lap and began purring loudly—an unheard-of thing for that stand-offish creature. Strange as it seemed, I had the impression they were old friends; and my visitor certainly knew the cat's name.

As I filled the kettle and put it on the hob, and collected some milk and cups and things out of the cupboard, I took a good look at him.

He was on the pale and slender side, and wearing a very long royal-blue coat, with a tall hood and silver buttons. The puzzle was how old he was. What little hair escaped from that hood could have been very fair, or actually white. Was it the innocence of childhood, or the long weathering of age, which left that forehead unlined? His eyes were a rare deep blue, but it was their amused, unblinking steadiness that held me—yet I felt no shyer of him than, obviously, Douglas did. Perhaps that was because of the lightness, or the lightheartedness, or just the light about him, as if he were on the point of sharing a terrific joke with us. As he glanced at the complicated wristwatch he was wearing he actually burst out laughing, and the curious spearhead-shaped stone in the ring on his finger blazed green and columbine red in the firelight.

Having made the tea and handed him a cup (Douglas on his lap, ignoring his milk), I asked him again how he came to lose his way, and where he was from, and who he was.

He grinned, but didn't hurry with his tea. It wasn't till he finished the cup that he replied:

"I'm a traveller from from a very long way off. It's not that I'm lost, but... it's a long story. Anyway, thank you very much for the tea, and your fireside and my friend here, and perhaps I should be on my way."

But I got him to settle down again, and told him we'd like nothing better than his company and his tale.

He said he'd do his best. And then, suddenly, from the side pocket of his long overcoat, he produced that fabulous thing. It came out small, a mere bud which immediately opened out in his hand like a flower.

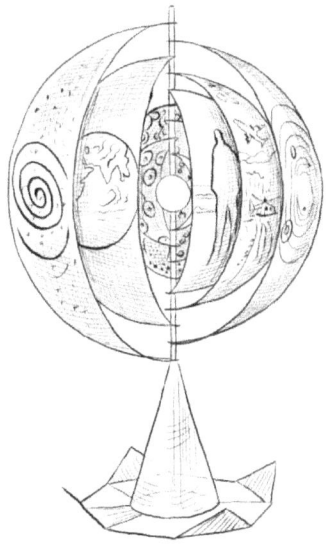

He set it up on the table between us. It was a flower with curious and gorgeous petals, an onion with bright painted skins and a crystal core, a ship-a-sailing with all eight spinnakers bellying in the wind. He called it his Deep Map, in contrast to the flat maps *people* use, and said that without it we wouldn't follow his adventures at all. He explained that it showed clearly where he came from and was going to, and the scenes of his adventures with the terrible Wormwolf. It revealed a living Space-dweller the regular astronomers hadn't discovered yet, and gave glimpses into the lands of the Gnomes and the Goblins and the Elves. And in fact it was a record of his great Space Probe, his journey to the very Centre of the world. He called this strange chart of his *Youniverse,* spelt Y o u n i v e r s e ; and he said it was his Magic Tool Chest, or Wizard's Bag of Tricks. Armed with this device, why anyone could ...

He stopped short. He'd noticed the look on my face. He *appeared* to be a human, and a quite brilliantly sane one at that. But ...

"Yes. You're wondering whether you're entertaining an angel— or is it a devil?—unawares, or more likely a refugee from some institution. Well, wait till you've heard me. And don't hold me to the *details* of my story. If they often seem wild to you, the facts they celebrate are, I promise you, still wilder."

I assured my astonishing visitor of his welcome and my keenness to hear his story. And I fixed him up with more tea and toast and jam, and piled some logs onto the fire, while he stretched out his feet to the blaze and began to talk, to the steady accompaniment of Douglas' purring.

Chapter 2: The Great Spiral

The name of my home is the Clear Country, the Land of Wide Awake, the Kingdom of Light. I've shown it here on Vane 1, the outermost vane of the Deep Map; and the picture is a perfect one provided only you approach closely enough for the edges of that hole to vanish— for my homeland has no borders.

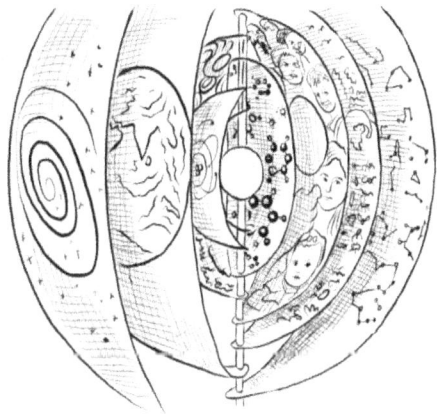

This country, beyond the reach of time, goes on for ever and ever, and everywhere it's such clear weather that no cloud gathers or rainbow forms, and so still that nothing moves, and so quiet that no sound is heard. In fact, if you listen now you can hear that same Silence, for it's always, everywhere ... Usually, of course, there are sounds happening in it, such as the crackling of these logs. But still can you hear, behind that crackling, the Silence of my home?

I suppose the endless Silence and Stillness and Emptiness were the trouble. There in the Clear Land, though I was as real and alive as you are now, I had nothing to listen to and look at (such as this fire) and nothing (such as these arms and legs) to look down at and *do* things with. And certainly nothing to cry about, or laugh about, or even grin at—I didn't even know what the words meant. So of course I got bored. And then, that music, that half-heard, haunting, mysterious music. That Song.

Where in heaven did it come from? From the Silence itself, the Quiet of that Land? Well yes, perhaps it did. But I was after a more solid Singer. You see, I'd got this vague longing for actual *things*— bright, interesting, colourful, noisy things that aren't too peaceful, and might actually make music and speak words and crack jokes and laugh and get up to all sorts of tricks. And I wasn't going to let go of that hope of adventure!

I just *had* to find the Singer, to hear the Song clearly, to understand what it said. Well, it was the tracking down of the Singer and the Song and the meaning which led me to discover this marvellous Youniverse, the Youniverse that our Deep Map sets out. To think that I might have missed it all, but for that Song.

I looked for an eternity in the Clear Land for so much as a speck from which that music could be coming. How long I looked I've no idea, for there are no clocks or calendars to mark off time in my native country. And then, just as I was about to give up, I found it, that tiny sparkle of white light.

It turned out to be the start of something big. For soon it began growing, and it went on growing till it became a whole cloud of sparkles, and the sky got dark around it to show it up. And it grew into this beautiful Spiral on the second vane of our Deep Map. And—yes!—it was spinning round and round, a great whirling, blazing Catherine Wheel trailing clouds of powdery light, marking out time with its great circling arms. Presently there were traces of red and orange and blue in its sparkles. How thrilled I was! These were the first *colours,* this was the first *thing,* that I, Prince Youlysees of the Kingdom of Pure Light, had ever seen!

Yes, that's who I am—Prince Youlysees, spelt Y o u l y s e e s . In the Clear Land itself, there was nothing to see and nobody to see it, so of course I needed no name. But the moment there was this something to see, there I was seeing it, and I had to have a name. It came to me out of the blue: Youly for short, or Youly-sees.

It came to me out of that blue-black sky which cradled my new-found treasure. No doubt it, the music, though still faint and patchy, was coming from that splendid Spiral. So I'd found my Singer! I couldn't make out the words of the Song, but I got the impression it was about spinners, about a secret all spinners share. All I wanted to do, of course, was to go right up to my Spiral, to *land* in her beautiful country, so different from my colourless home, and to learn there her great secret.

But she went on growing, and growing, till she half-filled the sky. Then, happening to glance around, I found myself surrounded by all sorts of other spinners, some of them spirals too, others snowballs of powdery light, still others like fuzzy flying saucers—bright islands in that dark sea. (You'll find a few of them on the inside of the second vane of our Youniverse.)

But I wasn't left to enjoy this Paradise of a world for long. That horrible lurking Wormwolf was beginning to make himself felt.

I wish I could show you a clear picture of the monster. But perhaps it's a good thing I can't: he would haunt your dreams, as he did mine. Throughout my journey I never got a good square eyeful of him. Like all master magicians, he was an expert at changing shape. (I'm not so bad at it either!) And with such an enemy you never know where you'll meet him next, and under what disguise. Sometimes he seemed to be a serpent or dragon, slithering and hissing and spitting; or more often a ravenous wolf, with his loping, prey-hunting gallop, and his ho-o-owl. And he was apt to appear quite harmless at first, until you saw through to what he was really like, under the skin. There's one more thing about him. I felt sure he never spins. No sense of humour, no time to play. Beneath his dignity!

Well, this time he had no need of a disguise. Was it a great sky-net he spread for me, like a deep-sea fisherman, or a huge web that this giant, hungry, hairy, galloping Spider tried to tangle me in? No! He simply opened wide his jaws and sucked, and sucked, and did his best to suck me right in, over his purple gums and between his teeth, all the way into the Black Hole of his wolf-throat: from which Hole there's no escape, ever.

Chapter 3: The Ringed Angel

How did I escape? Well, I'll tell you.

While that Wormwolf was intent on drawing me nearer to those terrible jaws of his, I happened to glance down and see, not these arms and legs of course, but instead a cloud of light. I'd taken on, without noticing it, that sort of body. In the Clear Land, with nothing to do and no one to do it, there was naturally no question of having a body. But here, in the realm of things, I'd become a something, and no doubt that Beast saw me as some sort of cosmic bun, rather like one of those objects on Vane 2. And it was this bun—a light meal, you might say, for a ravenous Wormwolf—that he was determined to have for his tea.

He got what he was after. I just watched my bodily remains slide between his teeth and vanish into that black abyss. I could afford to let it go: I'd merely taken on that particular body for a spell as the price (so to speak) of admission to the world of spirals and bright islands, but it never was *me*—not on your life! You're welcome, I shouted as I coolly shook myself free of all that stuff and sailed away like thin air! Ha, ha ha, can't catch me! No wonder he fumed and frothed at the mouth, and his eyes blazed like red warning lights.

Escaped from those black jaws by spacing myself out, I looked everywhere for my Spiral Singer—and was just in time to see the last of her. She had grown so vast that her edges were vanishing in all directions over the horizon. Filling the sky she was lost utterly. And in place of that shapely whirling form, here was a great shapeless confusion of whirlpools and streaks of light and dark, like the waters of a deep sparkling sea, rushing ever outwards, up to and over the rim of the world. A gigantic explosion in slow motion. Had my Enemy actually *blown up* my Singer? Is that what his distant howl of triumph meant?

Not for long did his triumph last. I heard again the song I thought I'd lost for ever. And even heard it more clearly than before. Yet I could see nothing like my Spiral, nothing to link the music with.

But there was one light that was growing brighter all the time. It turned out to be a blazing orange disc, and I began to be sure that here was my new Singer. New Singer? How strange! Had my great Spiral only been *pretending* to sing? Had the music been coming *through* her, and not just *from* her? Anyway, it was now coming through good and clear. No, not so good and clear! A nasty noise kept flooding in and drowning the music. It was as if someone were doing his damnedest to block out the Song altogether.

But for the moment my attention was held by what was going on all around. The whole heaven was full of stars. And as I gazed, admiringly, they began to enclose great shapes of animals, and of people. There arose a great commotion in the sky, as if an immense hunt were in progress. Look at this picture on the inside of the third vane, and you'll see what I mean. At the top you can see mighty Hercules swinging his heavy club, about to clobber—could it be a dragon, with a long snaky tail and a tiny head? Or the Loch Ness Monster, escaped from his loch and writhing about in mid-ocean? Hercules is upside down, but that doesn't cramp his style a bit. The Swan's wisely taking off to get out of harm's way. And the twins, Castor and Pollux, on the left of the scene, are holding hands nervously. And no wonder! On one, the Lion's creeping up on them, while on the other the Bull's pawing the ground and getting ready to charge. Perseus, the cowardly chap with the pointed hat, has his back turned and's pretending not to know what's going on, while the Bear's hurrying away out of trouble. Orion, a little more helpful, is trying to divert the Bull's attention with his shield, like a bull-fighter trailing his red cloak.

And then, suddenly, the great sky-hunt froze, as if some world enchanter had bawled, above all that din and danger, HOLD IT! And hold it they did, every one, for ever.

Let's go over to the window and look at them now, for ourselves. Down, Douglas, that's a good puss. Look up there! There they all are still, the Twins and the Great Bear and mighty Hercules and the rest of them, frozen in their tracks. And so will we be if we stay here much longer! This glass is icing up again already.

Alright, Douglas, you can come back on my lap now. As I was saying, everything stopped. But not the music. I turned to where it was coming from. And there, now very much bigger and brighter than before, glowing like this fire, was my new Singer. And around her a halo, as worn by saints and angels. And as I watched, the halo sorted itself out into faint circles of coloured light. A Ringed or Haloed Singer, instead of a Spiral one! Well, I wasn't fussy: her *Song* was exactly the same. Here she is on the outside of Vane 3.

And as I gazed and listened the circles grew bigger and bigger till

I saw they weren't circles at all but mere blobs of light whirling so quickly round that orange disc that they made tracks like huge rings. The tracks suddenly faded and vanished altogether, leaving only those beautiful coloured spheres you can see on the inside of Vane 4.

And all the while the orange disc at their centre had been getting brighter and brighter—and yes, hotter and hotter!—till, O dear, it quarter-filled the sky, scorching, blazing, hissing. … Something awful was going on. There was a frying-tonight noise.

And the Cook? Well, I knew then for certain who that sky-dragon really was. And I could hear him champing his great slavering jaws in anticipation of his long-postponed meal—of devilled Youlysees!

And I could see no way out.

Chapter 4: The Laughing Angel

It was sheer luck that got me out of that one—my luck and his dithering. That Wormwolf changed his mind and decided, a bit too late, to put me in his fridge for tomorrow's breakfast instead of his frying pan for tonight's supper. Result: he got neither.

On the inside of Vane 4 you can see part of his huge super-heated pan. And, half way up the picture, the next biggest thing—that streaky, icy disc. Well, this was his freezer. O Jupiter, was it in working order! I got close enough to shiver and shake with the cold of it. But then I found myself making for that other disc, next-but-one to the fridge and next-but-two to the pan. I hoped it wasn't one of his dinner plates.

Of course it turned out to be nothing of the sort. You have your own names for this creature, but for me she will always be my Laughing Angel—on account of her good looks, her angelic singing (yes, her singing of *the* Song), her tireless spinning and rocking and free-wheeling in heaven, her cleverness, her liveness, and above all her sense of humour. And here I was, Prince Youlysees, one of her many minor satellites it seemed, delighted to be dancing attendance on her, round and round and round.

A curious angel this, I hear you saying! No wings sprouting from those rounded shoulders, and not much sign of life in that rugged face! Whoever saw the mouth of the Amazon break into a South

American grin, or the Gulf of Mexico yawn a little wider, or Cape Gris Nez wipe its dripping nose, or Italy aim a sly kick at Sicily? Well, if you don't fault a rose for being short of arms and feet, or a swallow for not bothering with fins, why fault an angel for dispensing with limbs altogether, and for neglecting to wear a *human* face? Up there in the sky, they'd just look silly, or else get in the way. My Laughing Angel has *everything* the best and most gifted angel needs.

Everything! For a start, examining this glorious heavenly body through my magnifying glass, I discovered countless arteries and veins. They resembled the delicate patterning of a rose petal, branching in all directions. Some were strung out sparsely and others bunched together in great tangly knots. Many were actually growing thicker and longer as I watched. All the time new veins were forming, and old ones slowly withering away.

Now you may be wondering how long all this angel-watching took me. No problem! My watch here is a pretty remarkable gadget. With it I can take in or let out time, and make time run fast, or slow, or even backwards. On this occasion I used it for taking in time, and watched, fascinated, the veins of my Laughing Angel positively *snaking* over her skin.

There was another amazing thing about those arteries and veins. The Laughing Angel has, as you can see in her portrait here, a shadow side always, where her bright round face darkens and loses its edge and melts into the blue-black heavens that are her home. Studying this shadow side through my lens, I distinctly traced many of her veins going right on into the darkness—because they glowed, specially where they were bunched into knots. This sky-dweller was a sort of celestial firefly, shining faintly by her own light. A musical firefly. And a *very* talkative firefly.

It was her endless gift of the gab, as she smoothly coursed the heavens, which really excited me. And her laughter! Until then my Youniverse has been a serious—and occasionally downright solemn—place. But here was this Humorous Angel, roaring with laughter at herself and the whole cosmos. Or gently chuckling. Or, again, indulging in her own special brand of poker-faced, dry humour. O, I loved her for that!

(Laughter … static … pips … more laughter and applause … then:)

Comedian I: $%#@#**&^% ..!

Comedian II: *&$%%^$#& !!

(Laughter … Applause …)

I didn't understand a word of it. But that laughter! The vault of heaven rang with it. And somehow I linked that laughter with my Song. And I knew, without knowing how or why, that they shared the same secret, and that this secret lay at the very core and kernel of the Youinverse.

At first, of course, I could make no sense of her talking. For one thing, she spoke in so many different ways. But soon I noticed how, more than any other, she spoke this language I'm using now, though certain sounds like laughter seemed to be common to them all. It was quite a job learning this language but I did have my special watch to give me all the time I needed to get the hang of it.

And then, I overheard her telling the University of the Air (was this her polite name for her more gifted heavenly companions?) that she lives 93 million miles from the Sun. And that she travels around it once every 365 days, 5 hours, 46 minutes, 46 seconds. And that her waist measures 25,000 miles.

And so on, and on, and on, without limit. What *didn't* she know about herself, my Laughing Angel? And how fine her measurements! I never met a human who was half so precise. But I found it most amusing, the way she always talked of herself as "the Earth this" and "the Earth that" just as if she were not feeling quite herself today. Later on, I met a small boy who had the same curious habit, and kept saying things like "Bobby wants to see the crocodile" and "Bobby is tired". But how unlike Bobby she was—Bobby who hadn't the faintest idea of what was inside him, and knew nothing about how he began, and was quite unable to add and subtract, let alone do complicated sums to account for his behaviour. My Angel was onto all these things, or their angelic versions, and very much more. She was a marvel of intelligence (I.Q. at least 200, I should think!), and knew everything you could wish to know about her sky companions as well as herself.

However did she find all this out? I asked myself. So far as I could make out she possessed, besides all that delicate veining, no eyes or ears for keeping tabs on her neighbours. But in the end I found them, these very, very special organs of hers, some of them nestling among the veins, others sticking far out into space like extra mobile crab's-eyes. Still later I realized she had her own funny, put-down names for all this magnificent angelic anatomy, for her veins and sense organs, her non-stop talking and singing, the long fingers she nervously put out to touch and stroke the heavenly bodies gathered around her. She had this comic way (I guess this was really just another of her poker-faced jokes) of calling them TV and radio stations and programmes, and highways and canals and railways, and Sputniks and Apollos, and radio telescopes and observatories, just as if they were all dead things, happening to lie around. As if you always spoke of your eyes as Kodaks and your ears as microphones! Was she sharp-eyed for everything but herself? No! She just had a terrific sense of fun!

And she didn't always play this game. For here again, coming from her now so clearly, was the Song I had been on the track of for so long. No coy talk of Earth as somebody else, here. She was singing away about herself as a spinner whose secret, it seemed, was that she didn't spin at all. No doubt another joke. But one, I was sure, with its serious side. I was determined to hear that Song clearly and to understand its meaning, even if it meant circling round and round my Laughing Angel forever. Basically I'd accomplished my mission, unveiled at last that mysterious, elusive Singer. Prince Youlysees found himself in a kind of Paradise. And he intended to stay right there!

And then, of course, it came—the morning-after of that heavenly honeymoon, the end of that Eden—in a flash. Something hit me a tremendous blow amidships—or someone did. A blazing bright Serpent, with a long snaky tail, and a hisssssssss that tore and ripped through the quiet sky.

Chapter 5: The Studio

Cheated of his Youlysees egg in the frying-pan or the fridge, that Devil had just bided his time and come at me head-on when I least expected it. I fell.

My descent was at first quite out of control: the Laughing Angel exploded all-too-rapidly. But I did get around to applying the brake, and at a very interesting stage of my fall—sufficiently down to Earth to reveal unexpected details of her life. I was astounded to find her overrun by immense hordes of shiny legless organisms, with huge, luminous eyes and an unpleasant smell. I got the feeling they were poisonous and certainly they were dangerous beasts. Seen from above, gliding along their glistening trails, they were seemingly a sort of streamlined snail with brittle, bright-coloured shells, secreting these immense networks of silky tracks to lubricate their gliding. It was plain from their numbers and the extent to which they had modelled the Earth's surface to their sole convenience, that they owned her. What other species stood a chance against them?

I hung around long enough to observe how Nature had endowed them with marvellous instincts about how to slither along their often congested and narrow trails without bumping into, or so much as *brushing* one another (they were extraordinarily delicate organisms), thus ensuring the survival of the species. I saw their many feeding grounds and gathering places, compared the stamina and appetites of the little ones with the grown-ups, and noted how their numbers and vitality depended upon environment. In favourable regions they were strong and well-developed: in less healthy climates they were mostly stunted, sickly and ageing. I noted the way they loved to herd very close together, row on row of them, to cool down, rest, and meditate. I saw how, like elephants, they instinctively found their way to their ancient graveyards, at the close of their ten or twenty years of earthly existence. And I was horrified to find they were infested with big, four-legged parasites.

Just then I began to hear music again, and even snatches of the Song itself. Its source seemed to be a great big circular structure down there, with bits sticking out. I steered the rest of my fall in its direction.

There followed an interval—ear-splitting, confused, shattering, impossible now to figure out. And then—Alicia! Alicia, my very first human—well, flesh-and-blood human. So *this* is what the Singer looked like, after all! There she stood in that huge room hung all over with lights, singing her Song (or at least some of it) every word loud and clear at last. And, now and again, interrupting the song, a very aggressive young man in a short sheepskin jacket.

Alicia: Many spinners, ONE STILLNESS.
    Shshshshshshshsh. TOP SECRET.

Young Man: You're nothing but a painted top —
    a coloury, facy, racy topknot,
    facing the wind.

Alicia: Chubby cheeks or wan and hollow,
    rosy-smooth or pale and sallow,
    young and bright or lined and mellow,
    black or white or brown or yellow …
    Ha ha ha—little does he know!
    I'm the LIGHT in which faces glow,
    empty for the bright rainbow.
    You don't believe me?

Young Man: I tell you NO!

Alicia: Look, look at yourself then. Does anything show?
    Fly away coloured top! Where did you go?
    Many lampshades, ONE LIGHT.
    Shshshshshshshsh. TOP SECRET.

Now you may be thinking, that if Alicia was still singing that selfsame Song I'd heard the beginning of so long ago, at the very start of my travels, why she must by this time have become an incredibly old lady and sick to death of singing that Song. Yet here she was, young and bouncy and trilling away happily! Well, my magical timepiece had survived my fall in perfect working order, as this very same wrist-watch I'm now wearing. And somehow it did the trick. I hope this will help to explain how I was able to catch up with Alicia's Song, even after she'd come to the end of it—if you follow my meaning.

No ordinary wrist-watch, this beauty! But whose wrist was wearing it? The truth was that I'd taken on, not this time a makeshift heavenly body but a very convincing earthly one—the body of a boy about twelve.

Now if I were to tell you I was in a boy's body, or really was a boy, I'd be lying. It remained as clear and spacy here as ever, as it is right now. But of course whenever I looked down I saw a pair of marvellously obedient, jointed things like these I'm now stretching out towards your fire, and a chest and a lap like these (but without Douglas nestling there) and another pair of jointed things like these I'm now stroking his back with. I'm getting used to them now, but in that TV studio they were very new and shaky and hesitating. Yet I soon got the knack of giving these servants the most difficult orders, which they miraculously carried out in double-quick time. How, Lord knows! Here was a wizardry a million more times more amazing than any I'd managed in the sky. (Later, by the way, some humans tried explaining to me it wasn't miraculous at all. Do you think they were being funny? Or just incredibly modest?)

Well, I found these legs miraculously taking me into a smaller room, with less glare but full of noisy people. Humans! Believe me, it takes a non-human to *SEE* one of these creatures! Singing spirals and stars, pot-bellied angels laughing their heads off, the great sky community, even those gliding monsters—now *they* were, so to speak, *natural!* But these chattering rubbery things, punctured in improbable places, with their waving tentacles, were so hard to believe in! What made it more difficult was that most of them were doing a shocking thing. They were shamelessly stuffing alien substances into red-lined holes in their heads—and taking their behaviour very much for granted. Not a bit secretive about it!

They brought round a loaded tray of the stuff to me. Greatly daring, I put out a tentacle—a hand—and brought up just a little sample of it, and put it in. Not into a small hole in a head, I swear to you, but into this great big Hole I find here always, right where I am. And then another super-miracle: that shaped and coloured morsel was instantly transformed into—a delicious taste! How lucky I was! The things I saw being stuffed into *people's heads* had no taste at all, but entering my space they were quite delightful. I overcame my shyness. I warmed to my task, and soon that full tray was empty. I started looking around for more. Humania certainly had something!

Then I found myself standing, rather unsteadily and burping a bit, in a corner with three other enthusiastic eaters. The middle-sized one was saying something to me, and I couldn't quite get over the fact that the sounds were coming out of the very hole that all those tarts and buns and sandwiches had been disappearing into!

John: Aren't these snacks super? I'm John and I'm ten, and this is Bobby my young brother who's four. And here's Jo—sorry, Joanna! —my big sister and she's fourteen and a friend of Alicia's who's just been singing. TV programme, you know. I say, who are you?

Youlysees: I'm a ... foreign visitor—Prince Youlysees. Rather a mouthful. You can call me Youly, if you like.

Joanna: What's a Prince doing here? How did you get in? I say, are you feeling alright? You seem a bit unsteady on your feet, and your breathing ...

Youlysees: Well, if *you* were standing and breathing for the very first time, *you* wouldn't find it so easy. Am I ever going to get quite used to it? Or to losing jam tarts and things in my space?

They were on tiptoe to hear more, so I told the three of them— playful young Bobby and John so eager and serious Joanna— something about the Clear Land, and the music, and my search for the Singer (now located and identified at last, surely), and the ghastly Wormwolf, and the Spiral and Ringed Angel, and lots about my Laughing Angel, and how that Wormwolf parted me from her. Bobby kept laughing and clapping and running off for more cake. John seemed spellbound, listening to my story. And Joanna looked— more and more puzzled. I asked her about Alicia.

Joanna: Alicia's my best friend. She likes singing that Song, but I doubt if she understands it better than the rest of us do. But I say, are you being collected by somebody after this? What, *nobody*? Don't Princes have—keepers? Our Dad's picking us up presently and dropping us off at the Zoo. What about coming with us?

And then a plump and cheerful-looking gentleman edged his way up to us, and Joanna explained I was going to the Zoo with them, and he smiled and nodded to me and led the way out. He and Joanna went on ahead, talking earnestly and glancing back sometimes. Young Bobby and John and I followed, and we all got in a car and moved off.

How different it was to be *in*—to *be*—one of those shiny, slithering things, instead of looking down at them! The inside story was nothing like the outside story. But this was what I was always finding in my travels, whatever body I took on—car body, boy's body, walls-and roof-body, any body …

In the car, Johnny wanted me to tell him about space travelling. I explained:

Youlysees: I've never moved an inch. I just stay put and let things get bigger, as those houses ahead are doing now, and then smaller (look back and see what's happening to them now), or I watch them twist and turn like that corner shop, or rush up to and lose themselves in my space, like this road-surface. Now I'm gobbling up these lampposts just as I did those sandwiches, except they don't taste of anything.

John: Yes, yes, it's super! The whole city's on the move, sliding, turning, swelling, shrinking, and all the while I stay quite still. I don't have to do anything! That's magic!

Joanna: Don't be silly, Johnny! That's not magic. Real magicians do unbelievable things with spells and enchantments, things like turning your maths teacher into a toad, or getting your homework done in minus two seconds, or changing you into a beautiful princess.

Before John could reply we got to the Zoo—the Humanian Zoo— where Dr. Manley, the children's father, left the four of us to spend the afternoon amusing ourselves.

Chapter 6: The Zoo

We traipsed all around that Zoo till, at last, we felt tired and sat down opposite a monkey cage. I was quite sleepy after all that excitement.

Two chimps, one big and the other small, were watching us intently and gibbering the way chimps do. Well, I'm fairly good at languages, so I got down there and then to learning 'chimp'. It took some time, but my special fast-slow watch took care of that difficulty. This is the way their conversation sounded to me:

Big Chimp: You must learn not to be frightened or shocked by their crazy shapes. Remember they're Nature's children, too. After chimps, she was bound to fall back a bit.

Small Chimp: Look Daddy, there's one with its young!

Big Chimp: A kangaroo of sorts. See how she's *wheeling* her baby pouch out in front instead of building it neatly into her tummy. Hey, look up and you'll see, among those sea-gulls, another sort of bird. You can tell by its note, as well as by its stiffness and clumsiness, that it doesn't belong to the regular Animal Kingdom. And over there, mending the wire of its cage, is one of these creatures with a lobster-claw instead of a hand. And working on that building opposite are other specimens, with different sorts of iron paws.

Small Chimp: But Daddy, isn't it cruel to put them behind bars like this?

Big Chimp: They don't notice, they're so dreamy! But we've got them well trained. See how meekly they parade before us, getting quite exhausted plodding around their mile-long cage, while we of the Animal Kingdom just sit here at home in comfort, marvelling at the spectacle of Humania.

Small Chimp: Oh Daddy, I've just seen something *awful!* That creature's lobster-claw just fell off!

Big Chimp: Oh he'll be all right! Look, he's grown a very powerful sting instead, a horrible noisy sting, banging away. And his friend's suddenly developed a thick fur, and what looks like a shiny new red head and a pair of wheels. In fact, a very smelly and loud and fast and dangerous new body. Off he tears!

Small Chimp: Daddy, it must be terrific fun, growing and ungrowing any sort of body you like!

Big Chimp: I doubt whether it ever occurs to him, much less how funny or what fun it is. But *your* limbs, my son, aren't so easily re-grown. How many times have I told not to poke your arms into their cage like that? It's teasing them, and one of these days they'll take a bite at it. But now, it's time for dinner. Come on, I can hear our butler busy in the dining room. What a treasure that servant is—punctual, reliable, and so clean!

Father and son disappeared into the rear of their house. I shook myself and came to. Had I been dreaming? Dream or no dream, from then on I always saw the real human body the chimp way (as I call it)—a great scattered body lying all around the place like this toasting fork and shovel and poker and tongs, for quick growth and painless amputation. The funny thing is how these creatures think they're separate little living bits of mere flesh and blood, and never notice they're mostly steel and timber and glass and rubber and concrete, with dimensions and behaviour to match.

Well, there I was, sitting in their Zoo, as six-legged as I am now—four of them wooden legs—watching Bobby. He was splashing in a puddle, and Joanna furiously telling him to be a good boy, and Bobby protesting he *wasn't* a boy. He was a 'potamus'! He was a seal! He was The King of the Animals!

Johnny cut short that argument by asking me to teach him some more magic.

I replied I could show him how to unroll the red carpet for the world's V.I.P.. Or develop his magic third eye. Or paint the Zoo red in an instant. Or force things to wait on him like obedient slaves. Or take on any sort of face—animal or vegetable or mineral—he fancied. Which did he want?

Johnny wanted them all. I began by suggesting he should look at—squint at—the sun over the lake, and the glittering carpet of gold stretching all the way from it to ... who to but *the* V.I.P.?

Bobby said it came all the way up to *him,* because he was The King of the World. Johnny was sure it led only to him. Joanna said it wasn't a magic carpet at all but something to do with her eyes.

I said all right, but exactly how many eyes could she count, now?

Johnny said that all he could find was one huge great window, without any frame or glass, or anybody peeking through it.

Bobby said: Silly, Bobby hasn't any eyes at all.

And Joanna said we'd all gone mad, and threatened to take Bobby home at once if he didn't get out of that puddle. And then I found a bit of red glass lying on the path. Bobby snatched it and was soon shouting that he'd painted the clouds red, and his silly sister's face red, and the swans in the water red.

Joanna was very cross with him, and said he was merely peeking through a horrible jagged bit of glass, and it was very dangerous. He stuck out his tongue at her and handed me the glass and ran off to look at the wild cat—and, it seemed—start some sort of argument with it. The cat was growling and spitting at him through the bars, while he kept shutting his eyes tight and opening them again, and blocking and unblocking his ears with his fingers, and dancing about and shouting: "All gone! Come back! All gone!"

Joanna warned us not to encourage him. We turned our attention to the elephant.

I said: Look how huge he is, compared with the archway over there that he's somehow got to squeeze through! You can easily get it between your thumb and forefinger. However will he manage? Watch. See? Now he's shrunk to a toy elephant and got safely through, without brushing any of those toy children off his back.

Johnny was already making for the arch. He shouted back at

us that he was still as big as ever and was making the arch fit *him*. And then he began running all over the place and shouting that the benches and trees and animals and people were swelling and shrinking at his pleasure, and not one of them could do the same to him. How willingly they all waited on their King!

Bobby said "No, Bobby was the King. But Bobby had a tummy ache."

Joanna said it wasn't surprising, after all that cake. If only he'd quiet down he'd soon feel better. And why didn't he come and see this nice monkey with a blue face, that Johnny was talking to?

Johnny explained that he was swapping faces with the monkey.

Joanna said he was crazy, and they were a well-matched pair, all right. A pair of silly apes, with only a couple of feet and some bars between them. But Johnny retorted that *she* was the silly baboon, and in fact there was *nothing* his side of those bars, and certainly nothing to measure distance from. And then Johnny and I took Bobby off to the men's, where he was quite sick.

Leaving Johnny there to look after his young brother, I went back to Joanna, and found her crying quietly into her hanky. I waited, and then asked what as the matter.

Joanna: Nothing. I think you've been making a monkey out of Johnny. Of course Bobby is too young to see what's wrong about all this stuff, but Johnny should know better. This pretending to be a Prince, or King of the world, is just getting stuck in your babyhood. Little kids have to grow up and learn the world doesn't exist for their sole benefit. I think what you're up to is—well, dangerous. Fun's one thing, but …

I waited, and presently she went on:

"How can I tell you what's the real trouble? But then I might as well, I probably won't see you again after today. I'm *so* miserable! If you were a real magician you might be able to help me do something about my problem. It's my face. Oh I hate it, it's awful! My nose, specially. I've begged my Dad for a face-lift, for plastic surgery. He just gives me that pitying smile of his and says something about it's all being imagination and I'm quite nice-looking."

There was a long silence. I couldn't think of what to say.

Youlysees: Joanna, look at me, straight at my face. Now forget what people have *told* you you see, and just look for yourself. *Where* is this face now that you're so worried about? Can you find it? *Who* has it? Isn't your face *my* problem at the moment? In fact, no problem at all.

I got her to produce a pocket mirror and hold it out and get her face in it. And notice how it was around the same distance from her as I was, and my camera would have to be to take her picture. So all three—myself, her mirror and my camera—had to be say 2 feet away to register that face of hers. Because that was where she kept it!

Youlysees: Now you can happily stare in your mirror to see what you're *not* like! How's that for a face-lift—a really big, painless, instant one and for free at that? That's better. Now dry your eyes. I can see them coming back.

Bobby was quite himself again, more bouncy than ever, and demanding more magic. But just at that moment we were joined by Dr. Manley, who'd come to take the children home. And me?

Chapter 7: The Clinic

We drove off to their house, Joanna still hugging her newly-found secret, where we all had supper. And immediately afterwards Mrs. Manley, who never smiled at all, showed me up to my bedroom. She seemed to think I wasn't well and needed "plenty of sleep'" I asked her about sleep. She seemed very surprised at my question, and said something I couldn't follow about "losing consciousness—surely I knew?" I promised, as I got into bed, to try losing it.

I did my best, but what happened was I lay there and it got darker and the clock on the shelf said eight. And then it was light again and the clock said seven. It had jumped eleven hours. But I didn't *lose* and then *find* consciousness. I couldn't think what it would be like to mislay, and then come across, such a thing. Not at all like losing your pen or your temper, and their turning up again.

Mrs. Manley came in and asked how I'd slept. I said there'd been no gap at all between eight o'clock and seven o'clock. She just shook her head and looked even more concerned. I gazed and gazed at that lady, trying to make her out. She said I wasn't to be rude and stare at people like that.

When I rejoined the family at breakfast how different it all was! There was little Bobby stamping in a fury, and this time it was Johnny who'd been crying, and Dr. Manley was looking serious. As for Jo, she ran up and stood between me and her Dad, and declared she wouldn't let anyone take me away to that horrible place. The Doctor tried to calm the children, assuring them I'd be quite all right soon, and of course they'd see me again. Then he took me off in his car, with no word at all from Mrs. Manley, and the three children waving goodbye on the doorstep.

We soon arrived at a Victorian mansion that looked like an enormous three-tiered wedding cake, set in a garden you could easily lose yourself in. The brass plate at the door said it was *The Temple Clinic.* We went into a low-ceilinged room on the ground floor, rather dark and musty. But the people there were kind in a way—rather too kind, if you know what I mean. And they started asking me all those questions. Dr. Manley did a lot of the talking, but also a tall thin lady with hair pulled up tightly into a little bun. There was a friendly cat in the room, a manx called Douglas. And at once he jumped on my lap and sat there throughout, bolt upright and facing those people, just as if their questions were being fired at him too, and he knew the answers all right and wasn't going to let them get away with anything.

And they kept asking: "Who *are* you?" And I kept telling them I was a Prince of the Kingdom of Light, a Clearlander, a sky-traveller, a companion of bright angels, and—yes!—even a boy! Well, that was what I now *looked like* to them. And quite true, in a way, but not *my* story. And I invited them to come right up to me here, every millionth-of-an-inch of the way, and see if they could find a boy. Or anything else. But no-one came.

Then Dr. Manley wanted to know how old I was. I said, "Oh, at least a million, million years," and the tall lady told me to be serious and not cheek my elders.

And after that they sat in silence, making endless notes (whole books of them, I should think) and studying their fingernails. I used the time for looking at them. (They'd hardly looked at me.) Why were they so bent, some of them so hunchbacked that they looked all head and no eyes? And why did they carry on as if they were fast asleep and playing some sort of dream-game with me? The game of telling *me* to wake up, and pull myself together, and come down to Earth!

I decided they were bewitched, fallen under some wicked enchanter's spell—a spell which left them seeing clearly what was just in front of and under their noses, but blind to the rest. That Magician had turned them into hunched-up Flatlanders, incapable of looking into the world of our Deep Map, the living, many-levelled world.

At this point the lady with the bun led me away to a cubicle and gave me what she called a *medical.* She listened to my breathing on a little telephone, banged my knees with a rubber hammer, and so on.

And when we returned they gave me tea and some Lotus brand biscuits to eat (sweeter than this one I'm nibbling now) while they held a whispered conference. They were using grown-up words like *amnesia* and *psychosis* so I wouldn't understand. But they couldn't fool me! I realised they were talking about my medical and that *amnesia* was what I had wrong with my *knees* (which still felt a bit shaky, on account of being so new), and *psychosis* referred to my *breathing* (which still felt strange, like having to *sigh* all the time).

And then they turned to me again and asked me to try and remember. And I kept saying I remembered everything very clearly. And I told them all about the Clear Land, and the Living Youinverse, and the Great Spiral, and the Ringed Angel. And specially about my

Laughing Angel, and how intelligent she was, and how all their funny goings-on here below somehow went to make up her heavenly life. So that minding their humanian business was minding her angelic business too—whether they knew and loved her or didn't. And then I told them how I'd watched her spinning in the sky, but now I'm inside her (or *am* her) I notice she's perfectly still and has got the Sun on the move around her. Which is nice, and suggests she knows the Secret of the Spinners. And again goes to show how different things look when you move in and take up residence.

This seemed to startle the lady with the bun, who said I must have been to school, surely, and learned that it's the *Earth* that spins and goes around the sun. And she said something about giving me tests and perhaps sending me to a special school.

For some reason it was my Laughing Angel that seemed to upset them most—what had they got against her?—and they went off to talk about it in an ante-room, leaving me on my own. I ate some more Lotus biscuits. Then I discovered a box of coloured pencils and some paper lying about, and amused myself doodling. I drew a Good Magician with a hole through the paper instead of a head, and a great big electric lamp—at least a billion candle-power—instead of a body. It lit up a sycamore tree, which had to be drawn in several places because he kept moving it around without lifting a finger, by sheer magic power. And when those humans came back from their whispering they noticed my picture and said how nicely drawn it was, and they handed it round and pronounced it quite beautiful. Dr. Manley asked me what it meant.

I said it was a riddle-picture. You had to find out *who* that Magician was, and *where* he lived, and *when* to catch him at home, and also exactly what he was doing to that sycamore tree.

But none of them even had a shot at the answers. They just looked at one another with raised eyebrows, shook their heads, and muttered something about *paranoia*—another difficult word they thought I wouldn't understand! But I knew it meant I was a difficult kid, an *annoyer* of grown-ups. And what's more, I didn't care!

And then they repeated their questions, just as if they hadn't heard my replies. And even Dr. Manley sounded cross, and the tall lady tugged at her ears, and her hair seemed about to pull itself out by the roots. And someone said I'd lost touch with Reality. Yes, Reality! And it all went on so long that something dreadful started to happen. Oh dear, was I catching this sleepy sickness from them? I felt myself dozing off, as if I were tumbling into their dream, and about to forget who I was and where I'd come from.

But I was in luck. They'd no idea they were winning. They said I could go and look around the place. Douglas and I practically *raced* from that room.

Chapter 8: The Library

We found ourselves in the kitchen, where a nice old body produced some ham sandwiches and cold milk. After which the tall lady came and conducted us upstairs to a large round room which she said was the Library and Play-therapy Room—and, it seemed, just about everything else. Unlike the room below, it was lofty and brightly lit—by a big central globe: I couldn't see any windows at all. The walls were covered with bookshelves and wall-maps and charts and diagrams. There were scientific models, too, and glass cases with butterflies and birds, and a tropical fish tank with live fish like flames-in-water. And in the middle, a workbench with racks of gleaming tools. And she said I could amuse myself how I liked while she got on with her work in her *den*—a good name for it, I thought.

Her desk hid itself behind a bookcase with gaps between the books, so she could keep her eye on what we got up to. And eye it was—a solitary eye—all the while: those peepholes were so narrow. And she didn't even *pretend* to do any work of her own, for whenever I got up the courage to look there was that baleful single eye, blinkered between a pair of books, trained horribly on Douglas and me. I tried hard not to see as it followed our every movement. How glad I was to have that faithful puss at my side throughout!

There were hundreds and hundreds of books, many of them left behind, I think, by the Victorian gentleman who'd built that Temple. They were so interesting that I did manage to ignore for awhile that frightful stare. In particular there was one dusty tome containing a picture of an old German professor with the face of a child, peering innocently through little oval spectacles. And it told how he became so ill that he had to live shut up in a dark room, and could eat almost nothing, till he nearly died. His sickness had something to do with his dry-as-dust study of a world he thought was lifeless. And then one bright morning he went out into the garden. These are his words:

"It seemed to me so beautiful and true and plain that Earth is an angel, so rich and fresh and blooming, turning toward heaven her animated face. So beautiful and so true that I wondered how men's ideas could be so twisted as to see the Earth as no more than a dry clod and to look for angels apart from Earth and the stars."

Thus dramatically did he escape from that terrible Night into the Daylight World, the Living World. And after him came a younger German poet, a passionate lover of angels, whose aim in life was to be the Earth, "till she vanished into himself". And there were other poets, including a good, grey, wild American, and an English tailor's son, who revelled in my Laughing Angel. Oh happiness! I could bear that solitary, maddening eye, busy driving me mad with a terror of madness, in the company of such madmen as these—the *sane* ones of Humania! And Douglas the cat (you're sanity itself—aren't you?) shared my delight. There was a great serenity in that whiskered countenance.

And then we turned to the maps hanging all around that brightly-lit, circular room, the upper story of Humania, so different from the four-square and gloomy room below where we'd spent the long morning. There were aerial photos and roadmaps and air-route maps and shipping maps, and many maps of my Laughing Angel herself. All were flat portraits, with her features cut about and stretched to fit their flatness. And of course *lifeless.* It seemed that geographers don't record her music, her jokes, her flowers, or even her geographers. And what they don't record can't be important for her! The life on Earth can no more bring it alive than the lichen on a stone statue can get it up and moving—or so these Flatlanders appeared to be saying. Their maps, stripping her of living flesh, just show her bones. And heavens alive!—there alongside her bones were nothing else than the bones of one of these Flatlanders, his skeleton all neatly wired up and hanging from the ceiling, no doubt to educate and terrify the Victorian young. With his waxy, dead-white, grinning jaws and huge black eye sockets he could have been the King of Death himself, presiding over his subjects.

Nor was this the end of that room's horrors. Alongside the hanged gentleman was a full-sized picture of his insides before they were scooped out—a fantastic gutscape in vivid colours, fearsome to behold yet somehow less terrifying than the eye staring out of the ridiculously cheerful profile at the top of all of that horribly exposed anatomy.

It was dawning on me that these Flatlanders know very well that, homing in on a man from way up there, you come first to that neat, green-brown-grey landscape of traffic and motorways and town-and-country-planning, as shown in those huge aerial photos. And then to unadorned mankind. And finally to this gory butcher's shop of liver and lights and all that. Well, that's what they *teach:* what they *believe* is quite different, for what Flatlander, what normal human, rolling along that motorway at 60 mph, actually sees himself as a giant more powerful and lethal than any rhino? And what hostess, throwing a polite dinner party, wishes to know where the soup and fish are going? Or how many pounds of dung and pints of urine those smart ladies and well-groomed men are carting into her spotless sitting room, and lifting in and out of her best tapestry chairs? Or how much more of the filthy stuff her tastefully prepared dishes and drinks are now turning into?

Yes, everything around me said it: the most original and least noticed of all inventions is the Flatlander's knack of believing and denying the same thing at the same time, for spelling out in careful detail one story to the kids, and meaning and living its very opposite.

I came to the conclusion that Humania runs on double-think as its cars run on petrol. I was sure that Mrs. Manley, for instance, counting heads and mouths at dinner, would never leave out her own. That unsmiling lady clearly saw, yet was blind to, what she is. I bet Douglas that, refusing to view herself from outside as a frighteningly messy and complicated solid, and from inside as an equally frightening emptiness, she'd hit on a compromise, and vaguely saw herself as packed out with (say) medicated cotton wool. Poor Mrs. Manley, *stuffed*, like that Victorian parakeet in its glass case! What fun, what adventure, what wonder you cheat yourself of! But no cheating us non-humans! I broke into laughter. Stopped short by that watchful eye, glittering behind the bookcase.

Amazingly, this Humanian Library was proving nothing less than a Guide and Museum for all Deeplanders. For instance, next to that gruesome picture of the human inscape hung a chart of his citizenry of cells, the countless inhabitants of that once-walking metropolis, with all their nations and tribes and families, each little chap having a body to fit his job within that unbelievable city-on-legs, more populous than any Earthly one. And there was the picture of the great Tree of Life itself whose leaves were all manner of beasts and birds and fish and plants. And there were specimens and charts of natural crystals (no fewer than 6 systems and 32 types of them), a treasury of bright gems, gleaming red and orange and green and blue and violet. There were maps of my Angel's weather too, isobar patterns like some rough sky-giant's thumb prints smudging her face, and spiky warm and cold and occluded fronts like fretsaws hung with droplets of blood, scarring her delicate skin. And there was a whole forest of molecule-marbles arranged in strands and rings and spirals and boxes within boxes, many of them labelled, mysteriously, COOH. (Was it a Cooo! of astonishment at themselves?) And clusters of atoms, looking like sweet posies of daisies and buttercups and dandelions.

But what really bowled me over in that strange Library was a row of pickled human foetuses in bottles, and above them, blown up photos of human embryos and eggs and sperms. The labels, at least, said they were human, but the creatures themselves were more like reptilian, and fishy (with tails and gill-slits), and wormish, and even humbler than that. Why that horsefly orbiting the lamp was an angel in heaven, a genius and a god, compared with any human at an age of minus eight or nine months! I hadn't the courage to confront that haughty lady-with-the-bun with a portrait of herself at that tender age; but I knew very well she'd say: "So what?" The eye behind the bookcase wore blinkers, all right.

And yet this whole Library-Museum was shouting at her that man isn't only man, or even mainly man. If this was indeed a Temple (as its brass plate said) it was one dedicated as much to the Little People and Big People of the world (from particles to galaxies) as to these Middling People calling themselves humans. I studied those non-human beings till they were old friends. It was a long job, but once more this watch of mine came to my aid and I wasn't a bit rushed. Just how that unblinking eye in its den kept up its long vigil I can't think.

One relief from that relentless inspection, I found, was to dive headlong out of Humania into a drop of stagnant water, by way of the microscope. I plunged into a fabulous world whose inhabitants (though superior to that lady at minus nine months of course) were as unaware of my company as that toy mouse, which Douglas had unearthed, was unaware of his playful paw.

And then I stumbled on a deep but disappointing Dutch book, with pictures of a girl taken at every distance from light-years to ångström units—every distance but the one that really mattered, namely *zero* millimeters. The picture-maker stopped short with his outside story of her as *almost* empty space, and never asked her for her inside story, which (if she was anything like me) could have rounded off so beautifully his own tale. What she might be like *for herself,* apparently, didn't interest him.

It was this astonishing lack of interest in the heart of the matter which gave me the idea of making there and then my Youniverse model. I wanted to show, by including in it this crystal ball, the supreme importance of my space at the centre of the whole works. The Centre that is everything, and nothing at all. And I wanted to make a map for all Deeplanders who should come after me. A map of the Living Youinverse, which clearly displays the life *in* the world as the life *of* the world.

So at last I came to that work-bench with its vices and lathe and smooth-handled, shapely tools, and its drawers full of cards and colours and pens and brushes. I got down to work at once, and what I made you can now see for yourself. The pictures you see here of the Lower Arky (I must explain) came about in a curious way. Of course I lifted them from the charts and models all around. But they also grew into pre-views of the journey I'd still to make, to the world's Centre. My watch, racing on into future time, gave me hints of things to come, and so this Deep Map I built towards the end of that very long day in Humania turned out to be a sort of prophecy.

When I'd finished the job I felt as happy as I'd once been circumnavigating my Laughing Angel. What a deep and richly overflowing region this Middle Arky had turned out to be, after all! Long live Humania!—*if* you can see through its transparent make-believe. A big IF! All the same, here is a brilliant and many-faceted jewel, alive with endless reflections coming from all levels. Why, this fantastic circular room in deepest Humania already amounted to a model of the Deep World, requiring only that I put it in some kind of order, as I've tried to do in this thing on the table between us.

And so, calling it a day, I rested. I sat down by the bench, and contemplated the little world I'd made—and saw that it was good.

Chapter 9: The Observatory

And then, observing me idle at last, the owner of that baleful eye emerged two-eyed from her den into the brightness. Attempting some sort of grin, she examined my model carefully, and waxed quite ecstatic about how pretty it was, and how well I painted, and how neatly I'd fitted it all together. And, whether she wanted to know it or not, I informed her it was a true, a very, very true portrait of the whole of me, yes, of ME! And maybe her too! Other portraits leave out most of the picture. But she narrowed her already-thin lips, and I could see that my explanation was just an additional bit of evidence that I was ill, and now she was *really* worried. There was something awfully wrong with with me that I'd be the last one to see. The message was all the plainer for not being spelled out.

What I needed, she said, was to "calm down and be quiet and get some rest and a good sleep", and hopefully I'd feel better in the morning. So she led me up a spiral staircase to the room above, the third and topmost story of that peculiar Humania structure. It was, again, perfectly circular, but as windowed as the Library below had been window-less. There was even a domed skylight, through which the stars were already shining bright in a black velvet sky. She said the place has once been for star-watching, but instead of the telescope there was my little camp-bed for the night, rigged up at the very centre.

She went down that spiral staircase, down, down, down—how far I wouldn't like to say. I got into bed, with my Youinverse model on the table at my side and a pile of books I'd brought from below—among them Homer and Dante and Bunyan and Alice. And there lay Douglas himself, curled round the Youinverse like its guardian dragon, purring softly … yawning … yawning.

A ray of bright starlight caught the crystal ball at the centre till it shot out blue fire. Then—snow-muffled winds, far-off music inexpressibly tender, snow on snow on snow, glittering in the starlight all the way to the dark forest. Was that a distant wolf howl, again? It was so soft and warm between my snowy sheets, yet it was just as if I were in the open, at the clear centre of that huge starfield-snowfield.

And a fire reaching to the stars burned there amid the snow, crackling and blazing a thousand times brighter than this one, and in it burned to ashes all those notebooks—scores and hundreds of them—that Dr. Manley and the others had been filling all morning. And the roar of that fire became a great roar of laughter.

Then it all faded suddenly, and I was under that glass dome again, thinking of what lay below me, of the ground floor's miseries and madness, and above it the joy of discovering friends who understood. And now, atop it all, this true Observatory and Look-out, with its joy beyond description! Even in Humania! Even with that awful eye lurking somewhere in the bottomless darkness beneath.

And in the morning—how strange it was!—every snowflake had melted and the forest had grown light green and crept near, and there were flowerbeds and butterflies.

She came up then and asked, just as Mrs. Manley had done, if I felt better now I'd had a sleep. I replied that the night had been a very heaven of snow and stars and fire and music. But sleep—what was that? She stared at me, and her hair tugged at her scalp. But she managed to get me some coffee and toast, and later she let me out, on my own, to wander in the garden.

Chapter 10: The Garden

Out in the open air, I looked back at that remarkable specimen of architectural confectionery, the three-tiered Temple of Humania. I'd spent all yesterday morning inside that squat ground-floor Clinic, low ceilinged and dank and four square, where no one would listen. How different it had been throughout the long, long afternoon up there in that round and lofty and bright but closely shuttered Library, where so many old friends were waiting for me! And what a night it had been still higher, in that star-lit Observatory on top of the world, with all snow-bound Humania below!

But now was the morning after. The lady with the bun had brought me down, spirit and body, with a bump—down to what they call earth, two feet on the ground. Two dragging feet. Youlysees, Prince in exile, was feeling sorry for himself.

But the ground was green and soft underfoot, and a blackbird was singing. I wandered aimlessly through that mysterious and seemingly boundless garden, with its winding avenues that led nowhere, its secret places, its unexpected lawns and cavernous dark bushes, and here and there statues of humans. I found myself gazing at the lichen-covered figure of a boy. He looked like young David there on the mantlepiece.

Was I falling into their dream and becoming like that solid, clearly outlined object, just one more of them? Or was I still huge and open and clear as this bright morning air, ringing with bird-music? Why of course I was! I'd only to look and listen.

I sat down on the grass beside a gravel path, and scooped up a handful of small stones. From among them all I chose a little brown fellow with a yellow patch and just a dab of purple—never seen before, altogether lost in my world. But now its very centre, the hub of the whole cosmos! I saw and I heard and I smelt the winds and tides and waves and oceans and ice floes which had for a billion years been at work fashioning this precious creature just for me, and delivering him safe here at precisely this moment. For me to ennoble … But so briefly! Suddenly I threw him far, far away, never to be seen again! Abolished for ever!

What Prince had the power to confer and take away the highest honours like this, at mere whim? A Prince whose friends, the children, have been taken away from him? A Prince whose enemies believe he's living in an unreal world of his own? A Prince so mixed up he can't tell a live thing from a dead thing?

I got slowly to my feet and went on with my exploration of the garden. And presently came on a patch of unmown grass, where suddenly I saw—what could it be? Why it was a tiny gold star, a sun, glinting in the sunshine, gazing up at me out of that green world!

And at that moment a two-eyed, charging monster—all whirling knives and clatter and stink—rushed by, cutting its cruel swath. And cutting—Oh no!—cutting my beautiful Dandelion's head clean off. I picked it up and held it in my palm—that tiny, many-rayed, golden head, that precious limb of my flowering star.

And then, that voice, coming from just behind me:

Mr. Nicholas: Don't cry, laddie. I know just how you feel.

I turned sharply. There he was, sitting on the grass hugging his knees—a very tall old gentleman, in a long sheepskin coat. He seemed to know a lot about me.

Mr. Nicholas: Yes, I know all about your living Youniverse, and your laughing, singing, flowering Angel. And your journey and your magic and your royal power and your quest. And I know they don't believe a word of it, those … those *elders* in there. Oh, let me introduce myself. I'm Mr. Nicholas, entirely at your service. Come and sit by me. Shall I tell you what they're up to now? They're planning to feed you pills and give you shocks to make you *remember* who you are. But we know (don't we?) it's to make you *forget* who you are, and become one of them, a Prince no longer.

I let him go on, he seemed so friendly, and just now I could do with comfort from whatever quarter.

Mr. Nicholas: I've got it! I'll rescue you! I'll explain you're my grandson, and you'll say I'm your dear old grandad, and it's all coming back to you. We'll be out of here in no time, you'll see.

Youlysees: You must be kidding. You aren't my grandad.

Mr. Nicholas: Well done, Prince Youlysees! I *knew* you'd say that! I was only testing you. Now, I've got a *much* better scheme, and this time it's for real. Listen carefully! Your magic, your miracles, all those wonderful things you were doing in the Zoo, and many more besides—why, you're the only one who's really onto all these fabulous things. You can slip out of here as smartly as you slipped out of … out of old what's-his-name's Black Hole. You're a great Wizard, a super-Magician! You can make people follow you. You can use your powers for the good of the world—with my help as your Manager, of course, and so long as we keep our secret to ourselves. That's it then. It's a deal!

Youlysees: But that's silly! It's impossible! *Everyone* can do this magic. Even grown-ups—I think. It's just that they've been bewitched into thinking they can't, by some Sorcerer. I'd just like to give him a piece of my mind! He's struck them blind. Are you asking me to blind them some more?

Mr. Nicholas: Ah, better and better! You pass my test every time! But now I'm going to be quite serious and on the level. Listen. You've come a long way to here, through many dangers. And you've arrived at your goal at last. O I know it doesn't seem like that, after the grilling they gave you in there yesterday, but patience! With me behind you, why the world's at your feet. Humania's your scene. You've tracked down the Singer, heard her Song clearly. So now what? I'll tell you what!

Youlysees: But *is* it the end of my journey, my search? I don't quite understand the song yet. Who wrote it? Alicia certainly didn't. I suppose she really is the Singer. But … but I can't explain. Of course the Song came from her mouth. But what lies behind that??

As I went stumbling on I was alarmed to see the old gentleman's face growing longer and greyer and older, and his eyes bigger and … was it more shining? And I saw I'd hurt his feelings terribly. He looked as if he were going to be ill. But after a while he recovered. And then he seemed to have a sudden inspiration. He started frantically fishing about in the side pocket of that enormous sheepskin coat of his. And presently he produced a round thing that looked like a gold snuff box. Its lid sprang open, and inside, nestling on a bed of white silk, that amazing jewel! He took it out and held it in the palm of his shaky, long-fingered hand for me to see. We gazed, speechless. And when at last he spoke it was in a hushed but urgent voice.

Mr. Nicholas: It's the Black Opal! Your jewel! *Yours!*

I stared and stared. The low morning sun caught it and set it on fire. It was exactly the size and shape of this clear crystal at the centre of our Deep Map. But it had everything—everything!—this plainest of jewels lacks. Inside it, just below the gleaming rounded surface, yet sending out flashes of light far beyond the jewel itself, lay a little world of dazzling surfaces—flakes and flames of crimson and emerald and lemon and purple and sky-blue and scarlet—every shade and every shape you could imagine was there, and all of them continually on the move ... Truly I had never seen anything half so beautiful. No, not my Laughing Angel, not Alicia. I was entranced, stunned into silence.

The old gentleman had reason to be pleased this time. He held that jewel to my ear. I actually felt it touch me! And I heard a sweet lullaby, going on and on and on.

But then I heard, at first ever so faintly but getting steadily more insistent, that other music, *the* Song. And they seemed, these two so different themes, to be at war.

Alicia: Ha, ha ha—little does he know!
I'm the SILENCE from which sounds flow,
The soundless seed from which they grow.
You don't believe me?

But Mr. Nicholas, apparently hearing nothing, went on breathlessly:

Mr. Nicholas: *With* this treasure worn around your neck—your secret talisman, your lucky charm, your priceless wish-fulfilling gem—you'll never be sad or poor or defeated again, never low. Nothing will get you down any more. You'll be on top of things, on top of the world. *With* my Black Opal, Youlysees will be Somebody, the Winner, mounting higher and higher till he's at the head of the whole Higher Arky. He'll be way above this miserable Middle Realm. What's so great about Humania anyway? He'll be *super-human!*

But *without* my Black Opal, Youlysees will be a nobody, nothing, the loser, sinking lower and lower till he's at the very bottom of the Lower Arky. Finished! Look out Youlysees! I warn you!

I hardly heard him. That jewel was so astounding that I needed none of his frenzied persuasion. My hand started going out.

Mr. Nicholas: Your very own three-fold jewel! The treasure that's never *still*, never *empty*, never *silent*.

My hand actually touched that amazing treasure when I drew back, for louder and louder came that other message:

Alicia: Little does he know!
　I'm the STILLNESS that makes the world go.
　I'm the LIGHT in which faces glow.
　I'm the SILENCE from which songs flow.

And I could hear nothing else. I pushed away his jewel. And now at last even *he* heard that Song. My Song.

Terrified as I was of him, I was even more terrified to face the awful truth of *who* he was, to look at him squarely. He reared up till he blotted out the sky. He crouched over me. And I still refused to confront him. Yet I knew that face was growing pointed and hairy, and those lips were drawn back exposing long, yellowish fangs. Numb with horror, I was nailed to the spot.

And then at last something gave, and I found the strength to turn, and race, and race from him, his foul breath at my back, his terrible gallop. And I raced for my life to Alicia. For there she stood in the garden, singing still. And the fiend seemed to be gaining on me, and…

Chapter 11: Gnomania

But I got away. … He lost me again, that monster. But *I* lost Alicia. I escaped him in the nick of time, by … by space magic. You see, I rushed right up to Alicia as she stood there, singing in the garden. And, just as my Angels had done, the closer I came the larger she grew—and the less like Alicia. She grew and grew till she filled the sky, exploding and spilling over its rim, and vanished. Instead were vague patches, pinky grey, rushing outwards—rather like the streaming fragments of those exploding heavenly bodies.

I found myself in a strange new country. I can't tell you much about it, because the light was so dim and everything was packed so closely. It was like being stuck in a tube train in the rush hour—a train with all the lights gone out, and even more hot and sticky and stuffy. And bumpy too, as if everybody was trying to get on or off the train at once. I began to wonder if that Wormwolf had started to carry out his threat. He was 'getting me down'—down to vane 6 of our Deep Map for a start, or vane 1 of his Lower Arky. I was beginning to understand what he meant.

And then a voice came from somewhere in that murky confusion:

"Let me introduce myself. I'm Police Constable Luke—Luke O'Cyte. And what am I talking to, I wonder? What sort of gnome have we here?"

I looked around for the speaker, and discovered a dim shape, unpleasantly jammed against me. What I could make out in that noisy confusion was like a runner in a sack race with the sack pulled

61

over his head, or a blunted octopus, pale white. There's an impression of him on the outside of vane 6.

Well, we seemed stuck there indefinitely, and since there was nothing better to do, I tried to tell him what I was, and also (just in case he was interested) who I was, and where I'd come from, and how I was looking for a certain Singer (it seemed my search wasn't over, after all)—and perhaps he could help me find that Singer. And I ended by telling him about Alicia, and what a surprise it was to find that such a scene as this was—well, her works, her insides, her explosion. A very close close-up of her.

My story seemed to excite him more and more—especially the bit about Alicia: I could feel him quivering all over, and he started prodding me with a few of his tentacles. So I stopped. And when he'd recovered a little he started muttering to himself, and produced a little notebook and a pencil, and began scribbling away.

"Ooooo I must make note of this. How does this gnome— this ungnome—spell Al-icia? Pagan superstition. Capital charge. Everything it says will be take down and used in evidence against it."

He went on muttering and scribbling away at great speed, filling page after page—how I don't know in that crush, amid all that din, and with such apologies for hands.

It was then that I was amazed to hear, above the uproar, music! It sounded like singing. Could it be? Yes it was—faint snatches of the Song itself! But the Constable didn't notice it. He just sat there muttering to himself, and scribbling away as hard as ever. I asked him about the singing.

"Singing? It must be meaning those old vocognomes. There are some—bundles of them—on the platform."

All I could see were huge bunches of rope-like stuff. I asked him how those things could sing without any mouths. He said something I couldn't follow about its being the wind whistling past them—so draughty it was in that part of the Tube. Then we were off again, and he started questioning me about Alicia, and I tried and tried to explain, and he went on scribbling. Would we never get anywhere?

But suddenly he grabbed me, and shouted that we had to get out there. And somehow we made it onto the platform. But he still held onto me: and he was very strong indeed—he had muscles in that sack, all right!

And then all hell broke loose. There was a huge upheaval, as if an earthquake had thrown the whole Underground into total chaos and almost pitch darkness; and we were all thrown about, and I was half-choked, and bashed into all over. And *still* that Police Constable kept a tight hold on me.

When the dust had settled and the jumbled and tumbled gnomes had sorted themselves out a little, I overheard one of them close by going on in a very disgruntled voice:

"More industrial unrest! They'll be the ruin of us all. Holding up the community to ransom. Pulling in all directions. Oh my, Oh my! No, I'm not disgruntled. On the contrary, I'm very gruntled. It's everyone else who's disgruntled. Whatever's the world coming to?"

What little I could see of this old misery reminded me of a wizened and ancient spider, shaking away at the centre of an immense web stretching out of sight in all directions. But Constable Luke addressed him very respectfully:

"Mr. Neurognome, sir. What does your honour think of this? Look at what I've arrested. It keeps a-raving about some angel-goddess—Al-icia it calls her—who lives up in the sky and is the reason for everything going on in the world. It says all these upheavals and disturbances of the peace are only her twitching, or clearing her throat, or something. As Justice of the Peace, does your worship find it guilty?"

"Tried and found guilty of anti-gnomery, anti-gnomianism, anti-gnomesense, anti-the-lot. Sentence: lock him up in your police cells, gobble him up, and forget him. Quickly, Constable, before he starts talking to young and impressionable gnomes and sending *them* off their heads, too."

Police Constable Luke wasn't in such a hurry:

"Presently, your worship. My brothers Matthew and Mark and John and I'll share it between us. They'll be along soon. You know, your honour, this reminds me of a gastrognome I once arrested, in the course of my overseas duties. I happened to overhear him a-praying to—and a-cursing—this same goddess Al-icia. He was muttering to himself: 'O blast her, what cranky health book's she been reading now? All-Bran six days running for breakfast, and no bacon and eggs?' Yes, *he* tasted rather like All-Bran, too. I hope this one will taste better."

The Constable paused to give his forthcoming meal—me—an appraising dig. Then he went on:

"And now here's another of them. These cancer gnomes have to be cut off before they start multiplying, and then taking over. I tried to explain to that old gastrognome how I was a gnomad, travelling all over the Gnomiverse (even beyond the far Islets of Langerhans), and never have I come across anything but gnomes, all the tribes and nations of them, each gnome minding his own gnomic business and doing his gnomic thing. And why? Why because that's what he feels like doing. Putting through long-distance calls for instance (like your honour), or playing tug-o'-war, or eating away in all weathers without complaining, as that criminal gastrognome *should* have been doing, or ..."

Constable Luke seemed so carried away with the wonders of Gnomania that I decided to take him by surprise. I suddenly wrenched myself out of his grasp. But before I could get away (where to was the problem, in that twilight squash) he'd got me again, more firmly held fast than ever. He went on as if nothing had happened:

"All doing their gnome thing: the tiny ones, and the middling ones like me, and the huge and splendid ones like your honour; the short-lived ones of two or three days, up to the practically immortal ones like your honour again; those that sit quietly at home, and those, like me, that brave the terrors of the gnome world, picking up cancery intruders and basilisks—such as this criminal here who keeps trying to escape me. I ask it: where does its heavenly Al-icia come into this picture? What does she *do?* What *difference* does she make in Gnomania? Talk about superstition—this is super-duper-stition."

He paused for breath, that talkative Constable, gave me a vicious prod, and concluded, in a religious tone of voice, with a string of Gnomic Mutterances:

"Gnomo sapiens, the Flower of Creation, the Reason for the World, the Top, the Best, the Only."

There followed a long and reverent pause, in honour of Gnomo sapiens. Which I broke by asking, nervously, where All-Bran and bacon and eggs did come from, if not from Alicia. At this point Mr. Neuro took over the difficult business of my education:

"Did you hear that, Constable? It pretends not to know what every schoolgnome knows—that bacon and eggs are weather, climate. That this year the egg-fall has been disastrously light. That on the other hand, alas, it's been pouring jam tarts and hot dogs daily, with frequent lemonade showers and ale-storms. (No less than eight inches of ale this season as against the normal three.) That ice cream bars are occurring very close together—result: wind, and occasional cloud-burps and tummy-rumbles. The situation is critical. But why am I bothering to teach it all this? It's going to be gnomiculated—either for pretending not to be a gnome, or for not being one, or for asking ungnome questions—I don't care which. Be quick and carry out my sentence, Constable."

"Presently Sir Neuro. What I want to know is: where's it been all its life? Hasn't it ever been in foul weather, or noticed the difference between a mackerel sky and a pea-soup fog? Has it never listened to the Meateorological Office giving a Breakfast Forecast, or a Long-range Lunch Report?

"Talking of lunch, would you do something for us hard-working police? Tell this degraded prisoner your famous story of the beginning of the world. Teach it some history. Instruct it, entertain it, take its mind off the saucepan, and maybe you'll tenderize it. To taste their best these ungnomes should feel cheerful at the time they're slaughtered."

Well, I warned that miserable old Neurognome that his history lesson would probably make me taste quite bitter (I hoped I would *poison* the Constable), but he went on all the same, in a weary, history-lesson tone of voice:

"In the Beginning was Paradise. And in that Paradise of Gnomes lived Princess Eve, the great Ovognome. She was round and big and beautiful beyond description. And she was offered in holy gnomelock to that one among her countless suitors who should prove himself the worthiest. And on the great and happy day of decision there was held a Swimming Olympiad. There were no fewer than 300 million competitors in the swimming marathon; and the winner got, not merely a Gold, but the world. He beat them all—the fastest and strongest and sleekest swimmer of that immense and historic contest. He was none other than Prince Adam himself, the Great Spermognome, and his shapely head and long, lashing, whipping, shining tail. And of course he was the father of us all. Except for the occasional disease germ like this one here. How these horrors creep in from outer darkness is still a mystery."

I made another sudden attempt to escape. This time I did get clean away, into some kind of tunnel. But Constable Luke knew his way around that murky rabbit warren, and I was dragged right back to that history lesson:

"As I was saying, when rudely interrupted, Adam won his Eve. And the happy couple, now one flesh, multiplied to fill the whole Gnomiverse, the Gnomos. It was the Golden Age. For at first their gnome children were all happy and good and obedient and peaceful and understood one another, and observed all the rules of proper behaviour. But as they went on multiplying all sorts of differences began to come between them. Oh dear, Oh dear! They fell into bad habits and modern ways of life, and set up these dreadful trade unions, with their job-demarcation and constant bickering. They even started using different languages. Well, matters came to a head when they were all trying to build the Great Gnomic Abbey of Buckminster, which ended in utter confusion and Babble. And after Babble everything's been steadily falling to pieces. No gnome-unity at all. Everything going from bad to worse. Oh dear, Oh dear!"

"Well," added the Constable, "I hope *that's* cheered our meal up, and will make it taste better."

And then at last his three brothers wriggled and writhed their way into the picture, and all four started zeroing in on me, Oh so steadily and relentlessly, hollowing out their wobbling carcasses into great gaping, hungry mouths. It was horrible, terrifying ...

But at the last moment I had an inspiration.

Chapter 12: Goblinka

You'll remember how, in the Garden, I escaped from my Enemy by *running away*. I'd refused to *face* him. But I *did* face that oncoming gaggle of leucognomes. I picked on one of them and made straight for him like a charging bull. That's the magical method of the cunning cockroach, who escaped from his enemy the tortoise by rushing headlong at the creature and taking refuge just inside it shell; and living there happily ever after, feeding on the tortoise's crumb spatterings.

So I took my leave of Gnomania, thankfully. But my escape was out of mortal danger into a misery not much better than being cut up and stewed by the gnomic constabulary. If it wasn't their saucepan I found myself in, it felt at least like someone's food mixer, set at high speed. My first impression of this new country was of terrible agitation, like physical jerks jerking the whole world and especially me, with no breaks at all. I was exhausted already. This place was no better than Gnomania!

My second impression was a little more cheerful. There'd been no *room* in Gnomania, not even elbow-room, and you could never see much further than your elbow, or tentacle, anyway. Very close and stuffy, too. But here (we're on vane 7 of the Deep Map now) it was just the opposite—endless vistas of open space, paved in all directions to the far but clear horizon in perfectly flat concrete, marked out with white lines in great squares and oblongs and poly-what's-its and curving patterns. And over it all, a cold, cloudless, wind-swept sky, dead white and very lofty. This time no chance of feeling shut in. You felt lost in that friendless expanse. Not a cozy place.

The expanse was by no means empty, however. Plenty—much too much—was afoot. Everywhere, all the way to the horizon, military drill was going on, marching and countermarching in all directions at all speeds and in all the formations you can imagine—wheeling, charging, weaving and interweaving, marking time, reversing—all to brass bands, bagpipes, drum-and-fife bands, kettle drums, big brass drums. And everywhere a flutter of pennants, standards, ensigns, banners, streaming and crackling like pistol shots in the fierce wind. And bursts of rifle fire and machine-gun fire, and gun reports—and really big bangs too. As for the troops, there were divisions and armies and brigades and companies and platoons by the million, all wearing long button-up uniforms that made *them* almost invisible. They reminded me of those toy soldiers you can buy, all prim and stiff and glossy. And here was I—one of them! A tiny cog in that great military machine, grinding and whirling and clicking away automatically, like a horrid sort of clockwork. And all my fellow cogs—the troops—were very well trained: they obeyed the stream of orders barked at them by their drill-sergeants (moustaches bristling out of the tops of their brass-buttoned, be-medalled greatcoats)—obeyed them instantly and without mistakes. All of them, that is, except me—Private Youlysees.

I was in trouble again. For me it was a nightmare—a broad-daylight-mare—that immense tattoo on the bleak parade ground that is Goblinka. How hard I tried to carry out the orders barked furiously at me in quick succession!

"Lef, ri, lef, ri, lef, ri, pick em up, lef, ri, ri turn, lef turn, habout turn, make hit smart, quick march you hidiot, habout face, heyes ri, lef, ahead, by the lef quick march. I'll 'ave you court-martialled for this you 'orrible goblin, disobeying horders, pick em up … What the 'ell you think you're doin?"

And so it went on, getting worse and worse. The worst thing was that my goblin comrades—never an instant behind-hand or an inch out of line—were really showing me up. So it wasn't a great surprise to hear someone remarking:

"I'm afraid that old hobgoblin of a Sergeant Black means *you,* old chap."

The speaker seemed to be the soldier on my left, doing a ventriloquist act—I daren't turn to look at him. But *of course* that horrible black-uniformed barking Drill Sergeant meant me. I was always behind-hand, doing everything wrong, desperately trying to control this collection of—were they arms and legs?—thrashing about like the limbs of a marionette gone stark mad, trying to take off north, south, east, west, all at the same time. I wondered how I survived at all. My neighbour was very sympathetic:

"Stick it out, old chap. That ghastly Sergeant Black's off duty presently. You're a stranger here, aren't you? I'm Private H2O, that's my personal formula. But there are so many of me, all of us exactly the same, that really I'm General H2O, or Public H2O, if you see what I mean. Look out, he's after you again."

"Hif I catches you a-muttering Hi'll flay yer halive. Pick em up, lef, ri, lef, ri, lef, ri, Hi'll make yer dance a step hor two, ge hon with it, habout turn. Alt. Stand at ease."

I couldn't even stand. I crumpled, I collapsed—a sweating, shivering, trembling heap, and the whole parade-ground scene dissolved and fell apart with me. Those marching troops turned into countless shiny coloured balls, flying through the air in fantastic orbits, and I had the impossible task of keeping them all up and on the move at once, with that Sergeant still yelling orders at me. Their interweaving paths kept getting more and more mixed up, in and out and round about, faster and faster. Alicia's song, her existence, everyone's, depended on me—me juggling frantically. Frenzy gripped me.

Actually, it was my friend the Private-General, lifting me from the pavement.

"There, there, old chap. I don't wonder you passed out. Curse that Black devil! But cheer up, Sergeant Brown takes over soon, and you'll find him much less awful. Rest while you can."

When I'd recovered a bit I asked him where we were. He replied: "You've dropped into Goblinka, old chap—also known as UCROM, the Union of Chemocratic Republics of Moleculia. Very well organized. Everything under strict control: don't worry! There aren't only the usual military ranks, from Private to Field Marshall, but also, just to make things difficult for you, all sorts of nations and families and clubs, each with its own rules of correct military behaviour and drill. Do you really wish to know the details? I find it all pretty confusing, but then I'm a mere General-Public-Private. Now the DNA Higher Command, those great Spirals, know everything and have it all under control. Them, and all the other goblin brass hats—Myogoblins and Ryogoblins and Gobulins, and I keep forgetting all their names.'

I'd recovered by this time enough to ask whether anything else went on in Goblinka except military parades, and whether they ever went home, and who was the enemy they were all training to fight, and whether there was any hope of peace. His replies were vague. All he knew was that Headquarters knew what they were up to.

Looking around, I wondered why I could see so far. The paving was flat as an endless tennis court, without a tree or even a molehill, much less a proper hill; yet it was all on show, endless barrack-square miles of it, as though we were looking down from up there in that white sky. And those complicated blocks of soldiers, all those shapes made up of myriads of the same little shapes, sparkling and faintly emerald or ruby or sapphire. Why, they were like a watered-down version of that marvellous jewel I was offered in the Garden, or a shop window full of clear fruit gums and cough lozenges and polished-up acid drops and crystallised fruits. And that huge spiral building itself up on the horizon was a stick of barley sugar.

Private H2O warned me to look out: "Here's Sergeant Brown, of the great nation of Brownies!"

Our new Commander stood there, alone, in the middle of our section of that enormous parade ground, and actually *spoke* to us. Spoke! "Stand up and relax. Let Brownian Movements happen. You're not in charge of them. No—don't push it. Let your arms and legs, let the others, let Goblinka do the work. Maybe you'll get all ranks on the move and find yourself instantly promoted from Private to General, to Supreme Commander of the Combined Forces. You don't have to *wait* for that Field Marshall's baton in your knapsack: it's *here!* Just let go!"

And then this very remarkable brown-uniformed Sergeant himself started to move around on the spot, waving arms and legs, leaping, cavorting, turning. And we troops just followed his example. Well, I followed no-one's example. I just did what he said, which was nothing much at all. I got out of the way and just watched. I felt quite lazy, as restful as could be, at the still centre of all these goings-on of limbs, or whatever.

It was quite a discovery, I can tell you! Already, you see, before I left that Studio in Humania (where I first came by limbs of any sort), I'd begun to fall for the idea that *I* moved *them,* and they in turn moved *me.* Both so wrong! I'd conjured up their owner here, Youlysees ordering them about. And they just hated being bossed! Whenever I insisted on controlling them, they let me down. My movements started getting awkward, dithery, jerky, and oh so tiring! Less and less, in fact, like the movements of Douglas your cat here. You never put a pussy-foot wrong, do you, my pet? You're not beside yourself, wondering what some feline character named Douglas should do with his four legs and ... I nearly said tail! Sorry! They just get on with it.

Sergeant Brown made it so easy to behave like Douglas. And this was just as well, for my dancing got increasingly lively and involved with the others', till there was one single pattern of Brownian

Movements, with nobody directing them.

You can't imagine how refreshing it was! So far from even wearying myself even more, I was feeling better and better, till I'd almost forgotten that Sergeant Black's terrible drilling and grilling. Not surprising really. I was idle—as unmoved as I'd ever been in the Clear Land—riding Shanks's pony and taking it easy!

I was thrilled to find, in this of all places, in army-run Goblinka, such an echo of my Homeland. Was Sergeant Brown, too, a child of the Clear Land, and like me, on a visit here? Did he, too, know that this gigantic razzamatazz was only a close-up of Alicia singing? And that if we stopped she'd go silent, even vanish? And what about my friendly companion, General-Public-Private H2O? His dancing looked as unplanned as mine certainly was, and he did some spinning, too. I asked him about it, and whether he liked being the Stillness in which everything was happening. But he didn't understand at all, and just said what a splendid fellow Sergeant Brown was.

So I was left to wonder and wonder. Had every level of the Lower Arky, too, its secret members of that great Resistance Movement, beings who aren't under the Wicked Wizard's spell, Deep Ones who aren't Flatlanders, who find that inside they are exactly what Alicia was singing about—the Stillness, the Light, the Silence? I thought again of the three children, and that poor gastrognome who got liquidated for asking ungnome questions, and now this Undrill Sergeant, and my heart went out to them.

But no chance of revelling in my discovery. Sergeant Brown and his Brownian Movements moved away, to be replaced by my persecutor. This time there were drums to help him, and he was even worse. At first I got out of the way and let my limbs carry on. But Sergeant Black soon made sure that their Brownian Movements were replaced by Blackian ones: *he* gave me orders, and I gave *my limbs* orders, and they were determined to disobey me. It was quick march, quicker march, march me off my feet. To make things more awful, it got hot suddenly on that hitherto cold parade ground, and the hotter it grew the faster we had to go. For a while I did manage to keep pace and keep step in time with that relentless drumbeat—until I heard another drumbeat, and the two got all mixed up. And I began marching to another tune—yes to *my* tune, to *the* Song. And over it all I heard that Black Monster bawling, hissing, howling.

And it was all working itself up into a frenzy again, and again I was slipping, sliding, losing my grip, and …

Chapter 13: Elfanium

The next thing I knew was that here I stood, alone, in Elfland (on vane 7 of our Deep Map).

I was waiting on the verge of a wide highway, hopefully hitching, trying to thumb a lift—on anything to anywhere. Fortunately I happened to be at a promising pick-up point, near a four-cross-roads—all of which led, according to a signpost, to a seaside resort named Elf Ness. That, I told myself, settles the question of where to head for, when anything comes by—*if* anything ever does come by. At least I *thought* I said it to myself. But to someone else too, as it happened:

"Why head for anywhere? What head? Oh, sorry to startle you. I'm Elfreda—delighted to meet you."

And there she was — a spritely, graceful elfchild, a misty greenish creature dancing back and forth and around, too quick for me to see her clearly. And when she stopped there was little left of her except her voice. Or of me, except mine, I guess.

I asked her about Elf Ness on the ocean, and what sort of transport we were waiting for, and where she wanted to go, and a lot more. Elfreda replied:

"It's all a question of *making* something of your-elf. We're just waiting for somebody—some group or other—to pick us up and …"

The rest of her reply was drowned by the din of a fast-approaching vehicle. As it loomed larger and then shot by—paying no attention to us hitchers or traffic risks at the cross-roads—I saw a fast-whirling and confused pattern, like a cyclone at the height of its fever. But the pattern was made up of dancers wearing hideous ski-masks. All held guns, which they were firing in all directions; and they were dancing round and round what looked like a violin case, stuck upright in the middle of that crowd, like a stone idol.

Well I was amazed (and frightened) by that apparition—but Elfreda seemed to know all about it:

"That's Al's gang—Al Uminium. Did you notice their elfhoods? It's a case of an elfhood of any kind—you feel so left out without one. And Al's hoods are better than no mask at all—*they* think.

"You see, when you take up with one or other of these groups, they give you your elfhood—to their own special design and colour—and you're stripped of it when you're kicked out, or get out. Or *are* out, like you and me. Until we get a lift, get taken on by this lot or that, why we're nobody, nothing, with no elf-entity at all. As you can see for yourself, now.

"Here, look out: we may be luckier this time. Wave! Raise a thumb! Yes, we're double lucky—a pair of them! I bet it's Elfanium-B and Elfanium-R between wars, in a state of armed truce."

Two huge roundabouts, whirligigs of dancing figures, slowed down and came to a halt just in front of us in that wide highway, very little distance between them. And very little difference between them, either. They were the same in the number and the patterning of their dancers, in their patriotic music, and in their pointed red-white-and-blue elf hoods pulled down so that I couldn't see their faces—if any. And the tall flagpole that each group danced around sported a huge red-white-and-blue flag, and below the flag a red, white and blue ribbon for each dancer to hold as he went round and round the flagpole. It was like a pair of identical Mayday festivals going on side by side on a village green.

But, looking more carefully, I did notice two differences between them. The elfhoods and the flag of one lot had red, white and blue stripes with red on top, and the others had blue, white and red stripes with blue on top. And though their music was the same, one lot were a few minutes behind the other. The sound effect was unfortunate.

Members of both groups were beaconing frantically at us, and shouting:

"Hi you! Are you an R or be you a B?"

Funny grammar! Funny questions! Baffled, I started to stammer:

"Er, er, er."

But that was quite enough for them:

"Hey, you're an R, one of us, an r-w-b, a red-on-top elf. Welcome to Ephanium-R, to our great Fatherland, Defender of the Sacred R-principle! Come join in our national dances, and defy the might of Elphanium-B!"

And before I could object they'd dragged me in, clapped what I suppose was one of their r-w-b elfhoods on me, given me a ribbon to hold, and got me on the move with the rest around that huge flag in the centre.

I looked to see how my little elfriend had got on. I had heard her answer "Be who?" to their questioning, so of course the Elfanium-B's had at once seized and claimed her as one of their citizens. And I saw that, sure enough, she was already installed as a loyal subject of that realm, just as I was of this one. So we found ourselves on opposite sides of a great international conflict. For that was what we were now caught up in, said my new companions.

We took off—we Elfanium-R's—towards (they told me) "The Promised Land", closely follow by our mortal enemies. And after a while, as we spun along that broad highway in Elfland, I noticed that the music (which I was enjoying) was slowing down, and the dancers were growing tired and more and more out of step, and their ribbons sadly tangled. And it got worse and worse, till I feared the whole show would end in utter confusion. Now you'd think that, as a newcomer, I wouldn't care very much what happened. But I *did* care. Already I felt as if I *were* Elfanium-R itself, and its fortunes were my fortunes, and I sank or swam with my dear country. The truth was I'd gone a little crazy; for those magic elfrings are magical all right. Taking on their elfhood is taking *them* on!

And then everything changed. A trumpet sounded, and a booming voice announced that War had broken out between peace-loving Elfanium-R and those war-mongering Elfanium-B's, who refused to be reasonable and fly their flag upside down. So there was a state of National Emergency, and terrible sufferings were promised. It was quite wonderful how at once we flagging dancers sprang to life, sorted our ribbons out, and stamped and leaped to the speeded-up music. We were so together that there were no separate dancers at all.

Glancing in the direction of the Enemy, I saw that the same thing had happened to them. They too were now bursting with energy.

Their peace plan (no doubt that we should reverse *our* colours) having failed, facing danger and hardship, they were *one*.

I don't know how I got involved in the very first incident of the war, or just what the incident was. I do remember a lot of cursing and shouting and banging and biffing, and such a flurry of red, white and blue that the result was more like grey. It wasn't easy to be sure which were my dear fellow-countrymen and which were my unspeakable enemies. Anyhow, we warriors are apt to forget in the heat of battle exactly what we're fighting for, our sacred cause. But somebody, friend or foe, fetched me a terrific one in that scrimmage, and I went out like a light.

Chapter 14: Elfianity

I still don't know whether I was kicked out of Elfanium-R as a traitor, or was accidentally dropped in no-man's-land by the Red Cross. All I know is that somehow I turned up, very shaken, right where I started, at those same four-cross-roads. So, after all, we hadn't moved an inch nearer our goal, the Promised Land. What a waste of effort! I felt I could do with a nap.

As I gazed out at the road in a daze, it started growing wider and wider till it was no longer a road but a huge children's playground. And a girl—was it Alicia, now several miles tall?—had countless humming tops on the go at once, tops of many colours and shapes and notes, but all the same size, and they were humming her song. Some were spinning steadily, others swaying drunkenly. She was having a dreadful time keeping them all on the go with her whip—a job that was getting impossible. The worst of it was that if they stopped for an instant, she wouldn't just go silent, she wouldn't exist to notice it. And then something happened to take care of it all: suddenly every top was frozen motionless. It stood there quite still, while all Elfland revolved around it, and the humming went on all the same. Each top was the hub of a great disc and Elfland was all wheels within wheels, discs within discs, a gigantic disco! What a relief!

Someone was shaking me. It wasn't Alicia. It was my little friend Elfreda. How delighted I was to hear that voice again!

"So you're a war casualty, too! Ah well, we've lost our red-white-and-blue elfhoods, so now we're on speaking terms. Not mortal enemies any more. We're just nobodies again."

There was so much I wanted to know about her—where she came from, how she knew so much about Elfland, who she was.

"Tell you who I am? I'm nobody, a spacy nothing, thinner than thin air. No elfhood, no hood, no elf where I am. Come and see, if you like. That's not so awful as it sounds, because it isn't a sleepy nothing, or a nothing nothing. I'm a wide-awake nothing. I like being this way. Don't you?"

I was amazed at her words. And I told her that of course I liked it, yet I still found myself wanting to find a nice elfring to join and an elfhood to wear. And it was all rather a puzzle to me. And I asked her why, if she was so all-right as she was being a wide-awake nothing, why she was still trying to hitch a ride on one of these passing circuses—only to get an elfhood stuck on her that she didn't need or want. She replied:

"We aren't elves, you and I. Elves are known by the company they keep. Their motto is safety in numbers. Outside of company they're unknown, unelfed: and that's us, at this moment. Then why do I go on cadging lifts? I don't really know either. Perhaps my hobby is costume. I'm a collector of elfmasks, and a student of elfhoods. I like trying them on: if the hood fits, I wear it—for a time. The whole thing's a game—the great big HOODWINK being played all over the world.'

But I had something serious to say to her:

"Listen, Elfreda. The name of my home is the Clear Country, the Land of *Wide Awake.* Those are the very words you used. Sometimes I think I never left home; anyhow, I brought this space, its clearness, down with me. All this travelling never really changed me inside. You must be from there too?"

But I never heard her reply. For at that moment was a deep rumbling, and what looked like a black whirling sandstorm hove in sight. And as it grew and came upon us—engulfing us briefly in its darkness—and passed on, I saw dimly into its interior. There I made out many dancers, all got up in matt black and wearing tall pointed elfhoods with red-edged eye-slits. Every dancer carried a gleaming axe with which he beat time to a fearsome music. And in their midst I saw a tiny pale mushroom. Tiny, but growing all the time.

And as that rotating funeral procession—or was it an execution parade?—worked its way down the high road, and eventually vanished into the far distance, that mushroom grew larger and larger till it reached the sky. And it hung there in the northern heavens, a great grey fungoid mass, boiling and bubbling, edged in crimson and sulphur.

Elfreda, of course, knew all about it:

"The latest arrival in Elfland. Pluto—Pluto Nium, on his way to Hirosaki. Thank heaven there are less grim ways of making your-elf felt. Look at this lot coming up now. What a shining contrast! It's St. Elphis and his Sirens, westward bound for the High Rockies! Listen to that music! This is where I get on—I hope. Coming?"

It grew up just in front of us, and I got a close look into that fast-moving, thrilling, rocking scene. At the centre of it all stood a gleaming, polished column, very lofty, which carried, outlined against the sky, the white marble figure of a young man wearing a halo of white light, while at the foot of the column the Sirens—beautiful girls in fish-scale tights, with gleaming golden hair—were singing to a hidden band. And round and round them went, twisting and turning and leaping and waving at us, a crowd of the most free-and-easy creatures you ever saw. Their clothes looked like fragmented rainbows, but their elfhoods were all glittering white sequins.

And the singing of those Sirens! It got a hold of me like a rope drawing me into that circle. And they were so inviting, those young ones. They pressed and pressed us to join them. But—to my utter astonishment—I found myself imagining another rope binding me to that signpost at the four-cross-roads. For a while I didn't know what would happen, but this contrary pull, even stronger than the pull of the Sirens, held me back. Perhaps it was that their song and that dancing and the light that flooded the whole scene were *too* marvellous, too captivating, and I was after another music, another dancing, another light. I turned away.

Elfreda, half way to joining them and dancing already to their music, hesitated and looked back at me. I started saying something about our not meeting again, perhaps. But she only laughed, as they put her sparkling white elfhood on her, and shouted across at me:

"Of course we'll meet again, silly. Were we ever really a '*we*'? Two? Bad arithmetic!"

And so we parted for a second time, brother and sister from the same Fatherland. And St. Elphis and his Sirens wheeled smoothly away, lighting up the daylight itself, the dancers waving and Elfreda blowing elf-kisses till they were all merged in one silent dot on that wide Elfland landscape. And I felt, in spite of her farewell words, lonelier than I'd been since that wandering in the Garden of Humania, after I'd been taken away from the three children. And, for the very first time, I began to wonder whether my whole adventure away from Home hadn't been a gigantic mistake. Was it all worth it? Where would it end?

It must have been this doubt and loneliness which led me to join the very next group that happened to come along—or perhaps it was the music. A singing whose sad mood fitted mine. On the strength of that singing—so full of yearning, coming down the ages from the Great Mystery itself—I gave in to the urgent invitation of those grey-hooded figures and accepted the hood they put on me. Explaining that this made me an Elphian, a convert to Elphianity, they led me into the darkness within. They said this was the way to heaven.

And it seemed they were right. That near darkness—that singing darkness—did at once take me back to the heaven of my Angels. For as I got used to the gloom I saw ring upon ring of shadowy figures carrying lighted candles which twinkled like stars in heavenly procession. And at the centre of that star-parade was a blackness whose outline suggested a tall Gothic cathedral, all towers and spires, and stained-glass windows burning like blue flames. Incense drifted through the warm air.

I was given a candle—a star—to carry, and they made room for me in that procession. Overhead was no roof but the night, and all around this star-strewn darkness. We grey ones were so merged and lost in that boundless dark that we might almost have been hoodless.

As we moved along, a flow of lights, singing, I thought back on all that had brought me to this place. And suddenly everything was just as it should be. Not a twinge of regret. Even Pluto and Al's gang, the horrors of that Parade Ground in Goblinka, and the loneliness and terror in the Garden. I was suddenly so thankful for all of it. My Youniverse journey, my venture into the Deep World, was not a mistake or a failure. Out of that wistful, mysterious music a strange joy settled on me. A Youinverse that could come up with such music—they called it Plainsong—and especially with these Plainsong endings (I mean the twiddly bits that mark the end of a level bit), was Alive and Well and ALL RIGHT!—even PERFECT! And then, to complete the perfection, that Elphian Plainsong began to hold echoes of another music, of the Song I was seeking.

Well, that kind of beauty just couldn't last. The music gradually grew fainter, and then ceased. The darkness and its stars and the blue flames of those windows all faded in the brilliance of Elfland's broad daylight, that incense blew away in its wind, and there remained no trace of that Elphian mystery except this memory of it—a memory tender and grateful.

And so I was back again on the road, with little idea of how I'd stepped so easily and naturally out of the heavenly glooms of Elphianity into the full light of day. I was quite alone again—but no longer lonely.

Chapter 15: Elfbridge

Where did that high road in Elfland really lead to? Did that seaside resort called Elf Ness exist, except on the four arms of that signpost? I was beginning to doubt it. And getting tired of all this pretended travelling that always landed me back at my starting point.

And then Elfbridge came along. This vehicle, they told me, was really going places, and going there fast. Getting nearer every day and hour to that country where there are no more mysteries and secrets, where the *answers* are.

I was welcomed on board by a small figure wearing a full-lined hood with emerald trimmings, and a lot of carroty hair sticking out of it. He said he was called Freddy. Or, to give him his full title, Dr. Elfred Hairy Faery, Professor of Elphosophy in the Multiversity of Elfbridge. He explained that he had his very own special toadstool, though he wasn't sitting on it at the moment, obviously. And then, having put my new elfhood on me, from behind as usual so I didn't see it, we set out on a guided tour of that great merry-go-round—or serious-go-round.

We were much too serious to dance. We pranced, ever so gravely, lifting our gowned legs high, and bowing low when we met anybody. I soon got the hang of that prancing, and went round and round with the best of them to a stately music.

What we all pranced around, singly and in couples linked arm-in-arm, was the weirdest lady imaginable. Dressed in a crumpled white nightie, she was seated on a three-legged stool poised above a hole in the ground. From this cavern arose a cloud of evil-smelling vapour. It swirled around her head, which was mostly hidden in a mop of grey hair. On her lap lay a bottle containing a pink liquid, from which she refreshed herself from time to time. She muttered a lot and rolled about on her perch so much that I feared she might fall off into the cavern. My faery guide explained:

"This is our Elphic Doracle, mounted on her Tripos. She's on pink jinns, as you can see for yourself. (JI double NS, you know.) And when she not only drinks them but sees them too, she interrupts herself to scream a bit."

At this point she let out a tremendous yell, and seemed in danger of passing out altogether. But the prancing figures, apparently used to this exhibition, just bowed respectfully in her direction, and went on circulating.

Turning from the Elphic Doracle, I saw we were enclosed in a great faery ring of toadstools, supporting figures wrapped in doctoral fur-lined hoods and gowns, and bent low over microscopes. Their long, straggly hair was hanging down onto their work, so that in fact each was studying his own elflocks and individual hairs. They were very busy and never looked up at us as we pranced by.

Recently, my helpful guide explained, the two great departments of the Multiversity, the Departments of Hair-splitting and Nit-picking, had mushroomed into many sub-departments—engaged in curly hair-splitting, straight hair-splitting, fair hair-splitting, dark hair-splitting—not to mention sentence-splitting, word-splitting, letter-splitting, difference-splitting, personality-splitting, atom-splitting. The only things they were careful to never split, I learned, were their infinitives and their sides. Very serious they were, each glued to his microscope.

I asked him whether they still wore their microscopes, like spectacles, when they looked up from their work (if they ever did look up); and whether they ever spoke to one another, and why they made such a mess. He replied that the advance of knowledge did have its price—such as those greasy old newspapers that littered the ground. Research Fellows had to have their fission chips: the poor chaps had no time for getting together over proper meals. Such pollution, he agreed, was deplorable. But at least the Multiversity hadn't fallen apart or blown itself up yet—or if it had, we were dreaming rather vividly that it hadn't!

And at that point the atom-splitting Professor's hair suddenly shot up into the air, and he *did* look up, with a very startled expression on his face; but he immediately plunged back into his study, his hair still standing there on end, looking like an upside-down broom.

My faery friend was saying something about each hairstyle having its own hairspace and hairspeak, which made it difficult to know what was going on. But I wasn't really listening, because at that moment I had a vision.

I saw a poor tinker, a pot-mender, attended by his blind daughter. He was writing in a book about a man that can look no way but downwards, with a muck-rake in his hand; and of a shining one overhead with a heavenly crown which he was offering that bent man in exchange for his muck-rake. "But the man did neither look up nor regard, but raked to himself the straws, the small sticks, and the dust of the floor."

My faery guide was trying to arouse me, to attract my attention to our visitor, whom he introduced as Professor Doublet, Tudor expert and learned holder of the toadstool of Elfistory.

This tall, stooping, impressive figure in an ermine-lined hood had clambered down from the his lofty fungus and graciously joined us. And as we three pranced along side by side he stared at my hood and asked me what my subject was and what I wanted to teach at Elfbridge. I explained that there was one subject I knew very well and that was the Subject, Oneself: The Science of the 1st Person—of the Space and the Light and the Stillness and the Silence. In other words, I'd like to show those researches how to make *full* use of their microscopes, and stop overlooking what lies at the *near* end of them. They pressed me for more information. So I tried to explain to that strange pair of dancing professors exactly what I meant. And when I'd finished they started whispering urgently together. Then the Elfistory Professor began talking out loud, in a very alarmed voice:

"Elfred, as a Historian I've made a study of this sort of age-old superstition. And I fear we have in our midst a Mystorian, belonging to the discredited School of Wonder, Surprise and Astonishment—an under-cover member of the Faculty of Unknowing, banned centuries ago from this Multiversity. In his school a pass mark is one out of ten, but the honors go to nought. The teachers all wear tall pointed hoods marked D—D for Don't Know, D for Dumb—and they actually hold, not dancing but Duncing lessons. Freddie, you really must do something about this quickly. You know what. It's elf-evident."

And he pranced off shaking all over, that stooping Historian who told me I was a Mystorian, that Tudor expert who put me down as a wonder expert, a Nothing at all. He wasn't far wrong! My faery guide took it very calmly:

"Never mind him. Not liked in Elfbridge. Opinions, that's what he suffers from. Now me—I've no Opinions. I refer everything to the Doracle. So does he, of course, in the end."

He bowed low in that lady's direction. She was even more unsteady on her Tripos, sinking pink jinns rapidly and screaming a good deal—no doubt because she was seeing them, too. He turned from her to me and asked me, in a friendly way, to tell him what I was *really* up to. We had all the time in Elfbridge. And he asked me to speak loudly and distinctly so that the Elphic Doracle could hear too.

But I was still looking at the lady and wondering why she didn't *fall* off her Tripos, or ever *get* off it. I had an idea she didn't need to, because it had a hole in the top of it, and the pit below. But I didn't like to offend my guide by asking him about such a delicate matter. No, I was only too eager to obey his request for more of my story— though the lady hardly seemed in a fit state to take it in. Anyway, I went through my adventures in detail, all the way down from the Highest, through the Higher Arky and Middle Arky and the Lower Arky we were now in, down to Elfland and Elfbridge itself. I spoke much of my Laughing Angel, and of the three children, and of Alicia whose insides we were now exploring. And I rounded off my story by telling him about that Evil Magician who strikes folks blind to the

Deep World and dead to the Live World, the world I'd come through, level by level. And I explained how it helped to have a Deep Map of it all instead of those Flat Maps that people go by. And I said how good it was to find a few who weren't under that Spell, who weren't bent down and were able to straighten up and see it's not a Dead, Flat World after all, who weren't stay-at-homes but real travellers. I really let myself go about the Deepness and the Life, as I'd not done since that time in Humania with Dr. Manley and his friends.

After this outburst we pranced round and round the Doracle in silence for ages. Past all those splitters and sifters and pickers bent double over their instruments, till I began to wonder whether my faery friend had forgotten what I said, or perhaps hadn't heard a word of it. Not so. For at last he addressed, not me, but the Elphic Doracle herself:

"Did you hear all that, Madam? Good! Then may we please have Your Holiness's decision?"

She refreshed herself with a few jinns, hoiked up her slipping nightie, steadied herself on her Tripos, and passed judgment:

"Yes professor. I underheard it all. Hic. And I must sarraway that our grape and horonicle trouserseat of hic hic of elflearning is compisted off and 000000 mutterly disgrunticuled at all this speculyssees mystificity 000000. A load of hic hic hic of lodswollopy lobbocks 000000 fit only for nitwinkulers. What the hic does it stink this unitrocity is 000000 a hospistitute for manicle defectulors or hic hic the weeble menticulated excrementality? Smush it! Blush it down the stoilet paper clippers ... 000000 ..."

After a respectful interval, Professor Hairy Faery translated for my benefit:

"She says: We find your views most interesting. However, at present they hardly fit in with our current curriculum — not to mention financial restrictions. Therefore we regret we can see no Opening in this Multiversity for your undoubted gifts."

For the first time I glimpsed, as that kindly Professor took it off, the elfhood I'd been wearing all the time in Elfbridge. It was tall and pointed, and had a large D on it.

And so I was bowed out of Elfbridge, that Sledge-Hammer of Mystorians, that Bulldozer of Higher Arkies, that great Excavator of the World's Secrets, and found myself in the world at large—once more alone.

Chapter 16: Elfcounting

Back I was at those old four-cross-ways, that still offered to take me to Elf Ness on the Ocean.

Another vehicle of some sort was coming up already, on its way (according to the banner it flew) to the Great Elphinstone Festival. No thanks! Even before I'd inspected it, I'd determined not to get involved again. I'd had about enough. All I could see of this new lot made me feel how good it was outside.

Some were singing as they circled, some were playing guitars or drums or flutes, and some were smoking tiny pipes that stuck out through the hair that hung down over their faces. And in the middle of the scene rose the half-dome of a magnificent spotted toadstool, round and round which they danced, strolled, staggered, crept. I noticed that the rim of that fungus was uneven, as if the mice had been at it, or caterpillars. It turned out to be the dancers themselves. From time to time one of them would break off a bit of the toadstool and nibble it. And a few were lying flat on their backs, staring up at the sky. Had they found their own way of seeing into the Deep World? They didn't look to me like Flatlanders. Funny people though they were, they were not bowed down. And their music was nice, too— much nicer than the smoke that came out of their little elfin pipes.

And so they, and their strange smell, went with the wind, and I was left to wonder how to get off this road, out of Elfland altogether. Anyhow I wasn't going to be elf hoodwinked anymore.

But I had no choice. The next thing I knew I was being forcibly dragged in—into this Elf-counter Group.

I hadn't even noticed their arrival at the cross roads, I was so deep in my schemes about how to get away. It came as a shock to find myself being roughly shaken by a tall athletic character in a long sheepskin with a hood, buttoned up so high that I couldn't see his face. He kept trying to tell me I had a bad-elf problem, and we were going to work on it. Well, he was much stronger than me, and in the end he practically knocked me out. And when I came to he was carting me along into his circle, where he plonked me down on a puffball in a whole ring of puffballs, most of them occupied. He sat himself down on a big fungus at the centre, and started to explain that what we were after wasn't just elfhood: it was super-elfhood. But since this was an Elf-counter Group we had to start from the beginning by counting, counting our elfhoods. He pointed to a young fellow on my left, and we started off.

"One. Two. Three. Four."

It was my turn. I said: "PASS!"

I thought our leader would do himself—or me—an injury, he was so wild. Shaking his finger at me, he warned me to be serious, and we began again. Were we all present and correct?

"One. Two. Three. Four."

"Quite correct. But ABSENT! Just room for everyone." I was just being truthful, reporting what I saw.

I think our Leader did actually hurt himself this time. But after a while he pulled himself together enough to splutter something about my being a sub-elf instead of a super-elf, and my having an elf problem far worse than he'd feared. And he yelled FIVE on my behalf, and the others counted on, up to a total of twelve — which, with him in the middle added in, came to thirteen elfhoods in all. Well, I still made it only twelve, and I checked it privately by pointing at each one in turn, and counting exactly what I saw.

Our Leader caught me at it, and explained to the others that my mental age was about three. But instead of throwing me out, he went on to say that our next step in this workshop was to go round the circle introducing ourselves. Name, job, how we saw ourselves—in a nutshell.

Number One said he was Robin Hood, and he'd come along with his sister, Riding. His job was archery and sheriff baiting and lightening the purses of abbots. And he was green, of course.

(I daren't say anything, but Robin's hood was reddish. No-one else seemed to notice, or care.) It was his sister's turn:

"I'm a very well-behaved little girl, except that I do wander from the path, picking flowers and getting into trouble with strangers. And my hood's bright red, as everybody knows. But I do have a Grandma problem. And—oh dear!—I think it's coming up now."

She was staring at our Leader as if she'd seen ghost. But he settled deep into his sheepskin and succeeded in calming her a little. The round of introductions continued:

Number Three said: "My name is King Cole, and black is beautiful."

Number Four said: "I'm Mr. Cole's girl-friend and my name is

Daisy Dazz and I'm whiter than white."

As the couple gazed soulfully at each other I saw that, actually, they'd got things the wrong way round: her elfhood was black, and his was white. But again I said nothing. And—panic—my turn had come round!

"I … I …"

I gave up. And I ran for it—from *him*. For at last I'd faced the truth, I'd seen who he was inside the sheepskin.

But he was up and after me. At my back that dreadful footfall— and that hooowl.

Chapter 17:
The New Clear Land

This time I ran faster than he did. I heard him actually falling behind, howling his rage further and further behind till I lost him and his howling altogether, and could safely slow down. For the moment I'd escaped from my Enemy. And from Elfland, too—at last! But escaped to where?

It was hard to say, as yet. On our Deep Map I was on vane 9, the very last one. I looked all round—into nothing. Out of nothing here into nothing there, and a very peculiar feeling it gave me: one that took me back into long ago. So much of this nothing there was, stretching to the horizon that should have been there, but wasn't. It was almost like being at home in the Clear Land again.

But not quite. Occasional distant swishes, and blips, and crashes, pierced the calm of that place; and rushes of sound like the whine of invisible jets, or waves breaking on remote bewitched seashores, or some giant Troll running his horny finger round the world's rim and clicking his tongue. It was eerie. It didn't feel very safe here, in this new Clear Land. Sometimes those swish-pasts became roar-pasts, and showed they meant business by leaving behind long feathery vapour-trails, curving, straight, occasionally colliding and cancelling each other out—till that vast skyscape was a giant cat's cradle of them. Often I thought I was really being run down (not deliberately, I hope). And I'm sure that once that invisible rushing actually went clean through me. Strangely enough, it didn't seem to do me any harm — but I did feel dreadfully shaken.

The worst of it was that there was nothing I could do, and nowhere to go, and no chance of getting out of harm's way. These nasty things came at you anyway and from anywhere. I could only wait and see. Or see and wait—which I find to be a better idea, if you follow me.

And then that voice:

"If you wait long enough, you'll see the Great Jubilee Parade."

That small voice, coming from almost no-one and almost nowhere, but so familiar! And O so very, very welcome!

"Elfreda!"

"No, just Freda. We aren't elves anymore, thank goodness!"

"But, Elfeda—I mean Freda—where are we?"

"Just where you thought. This is the New Clear Land. Some say it's done away with the Old Clear Land for ever, and it's a great improvement: it's our Real Homeland, they say—that other place is just Make Believe. Anyway, I think you'll enjoy the Great Tickle Parade. Look!"

Leading the procession was a lumbering float carrying an enormous crown made of tinsel and silver paper, and studded with chunks of broken glass for jewels. Beneath this royal headgear was a tangled mop of finely split hair—hair curly and straight and fair and dark—but no sovereign's head or body supporting that mass. It looked very hastily put together, and rather shaky, but the overall effect was impressive. The top-most gems of that royal diadem reached out of sight. Freda explained:

"That's the Emperor and High Priest of the New Clear Land, the reigning head of the Pothesis Dynasty. They call him the Latest High Pothesis, and he rules with a rod of … of Uranium. It's his 80th anniversary.

"And that's Pa Tickle—Old Proton they call him—leading his family on his tandem. The lady behind him—I bet she's doing all the pedalling—is his wife Neutrona. And that third one, going round and round her Pa and Ma, is Electra. You see how swift and straight-backed Electra is, spinning away on her little moped, head up there in the clouds. She likes to be called Miss Tickle: she spends ages in her private cloud chamber, having beautiful experiences."

And on and on they came, that strange and vivacious Tickle family, hundreds of them, mounted on push-bikes and tricycles and tandems and two-stroke mopeds and racing motorbikes. Some of them were as ponderous as old Pa himself. Others were as light and nimble as Electra. And some of them were very short-lived—they suddenly vanished into thin air! Others seemed to go on for ever. But they were all laughing their heads off (they had none left that I could see), and bursting with energy, and waving so rapidly that you could hardly see them for waves. The whole Parade might have been one tremendous wave. Freda managed to pick out quite a few characters she knew. But there were a lot of strange ones she hadn't met before.

Then came a very noisy spectacle. My first impression was of a great Catherine Wheel on its side. It turned out to be a circular cycle-track, round which hundreds of motorbikes were roaring and screeching, getting up such fabulous speeds that eventually they shot off into space, leaving behind them bubbling vapour trails. The whole thing reminded me of the very first object I ever saw, that great Spiral Angel, spinning so quietly in the heavens. I wished this version were like that.

But the end of the procession was already in sight. Bringing up the rear was a huge and chaotic pack of the oddest little animals. It was impossible to make head or tail or even middle of them, they moved so fast, snuffling and hunting about in all directions. From the noise they were making, I got the impression that they'd started life unsure whether to be puppies or ducklings, and so turned out to be half dog and half duck. For they were neither quacking nor barking, but quarking. I fancied them to be four-legged, with feathers instead of hair, and snapping beaks—something like bad-tempered Duckbilled Platypuses. I shared these impressions with Freda. She replied:

"I doubt whether they're such a rabble as you'd think, those creatures. More like a pack of hounds. Is it their Master in the far distance, urging them on, and conducting the whole Parade from the rear?"

I couldn't see any Master of hounds, and turned my attention to the great Tickle family. All of them were waving and roaring with laughter. And some of this waving, surely, was directed at Freda and me. They seemed to be inviting us to join them on parade before it was too late. I didn't need any persuasion. These creatures—I knew it!—had something I didn't, a secret I needed to uncover while I still had the chance. Well, there was only one way to do that—by joining in at once. Freda agreed enthusiastically.

But it wasn't so easy. We hit an invisible wall whenever we tried to get into that procession. And then, in an instant, we were right there amongst them! We'd jumped clean over (or through) that wall in a magic leap from A to Z—*without ever going through B, C, D, and so on!* There's acrobatics for you!

How they welcomed us! How perfectly we fitted in! We found ourselves waving and dancing and flinging ourselves around with as much abandon as any of them. They didn't tell us their secret was UNCERTAINTY—they got on with it, they were it, and we caught it from them. None of us had the slightest idea what would happen next. Was I just about to spin like a top, or turn cartwheels, or do the high jump, or the long jump, or shout, or sing? The only way to find out was to watch and see what I actually got up to.

I couldn't believe the difference it made—this entry into NOW, this freedom from the dead hand of an imaginary future. I felt so carefree, so alive, so adventurous: it was like a great wind blowing through me, blowing clean away all my plotting and planning mind, left over from Humania. I just went blank, clueless. An alert idiot— that was me! Result: a million, million possibilities opened out, nothing was impossible, because that whole scene in the New Clear Land, the great world itself, was new every moment, unforeseeable, anybody's guess, bursting with marvels. Each instant was a brand new start, the creation of the world out of nothing at all. Oh the relief, the letting go, the fun, the freedom, yes the bliss, that suddenly came to me on that strangest of parades, when I exchanged INTENTION for ATTENTION! Every gesture was so beautiful, so right. I couldn't put a foot wrong. Nor could Freda, nor could any of us. This absence of any future mysteriously took care of what the present came up with. With reverence, we watched the dance unfold.

And how astonishing—yet how fitting—to have found here, of all places, at what turned out to be the very lowest point of the Lower Arky, that hidden truth: freedom is built into the Youniverse, lies at its base, is its base, its very foundation, *now*. Only by going down so far, through so many strange countries to this strangest of them all, could I have unearthed this deepest of secrets.

The dancing was all surprises; Freda's grace and inventiveness amazed me; her laughter rang and rang through that land. And in and above it all came snatches of ... of that music, of my music, of the music .

It was one of the finest moments of my whole adventure!

Chapter 18:
The Cone and the Dungeon

I must have taken on some sort of a body when I joined that great parade in the New Clear Land—no doubt a lightsome wisp of a one like my companions'. At first it worked so well I didn't know it existed, but soon it announced itself—by flagging. It had some of their astonishing energy but none of their staying-power. I found myself tiring, stumbling, less and less able to keep up with Freda and the rest. I called out to them, but they were already out of earshot. I fell further and further behind, till the last of them had dwindled to nothing, and I was left on my own—alone.

Alone—except for that yelping pack of Quarks behind me. Louder and louder their quarking, more and more threatening. And worse: dominating their cries another well-remembered cry, coming from the Master of those foxhounds, from that dread Hunter.

Terror of him sapping the last of my energy, my very life ebbing away with every movement, I was being chased through emptiness into more emptiness, with nowhere to turn. But worse was to come.

The emptiness ahead was actually closing in on me. I found myself in an ever-narrowing tunnel, a cone, heading straight for the point at the dead end of it. No exit. I was caught in that relentless Hunter's snare, his giant fish-trap, his butterfly-net, his duck-decoy. And then, in an instant, I was halted—stopped dead, held rigid, frozen into a block of ice.

Was this dead end Death itself? Of that baying pack I heard no more. No need of them now. Their Master had won. He'd chased me through every level of this Youniverse, only to catch me at last in his icy death-trap at the bottom of it all. I knew I was finished—for there was nowhere else to go. Could this, after all, be the core of the Youniverse I'd discovered—the place where all hope is abandoned?

His gruesome laughter came from just behind me. But close or far—what did it matter now? It was all over. In my icy dungeon I was dumb: even my voice was frozen into silence. But that ice produced no numbness to deaden me to the pain of defeat. His power over me was so complete that his old hunting fury had no point now. It was enough for him to play with me, to gloat, in a voice that was almost gentle—as torturers can be to their victims when they have all the time in the world to mangle and twist and probe.

He talked. And while he talked—*at* me, not *to* me—he frolicked and howled and gambolled round and round my ice-prison, kicking his heels high, leering in at me as he passed. Not that I could see him clearly—even if I'd dared to. It was like looking out through a flood of tears—tears of ice—for the walls of my prison turned his grin, his whole body into distorted, ballooning shapes—more horrible than any fairground mirror ever could.

"Let me welcome him to his new home, my White Hole. O it fits him like an iron glove. Much tighter than my Black Hole would have done. Does he remember how he laughed at *me*—at me—when he managed to slip out of that hole in the sky? The laugh's on him now. There'd have been sleep for him in that warm blackness: here, not a wink. He side-stepped my very first trap, only to find himself in my very last trap, my really cruel one, my Deepest Freeze. He did me out of my dinner then—but now I have him safely on ice. I'll wolf him! No hurry, my little ice-cream lollipop's ready for just when I fancy him."

Then that creature drew to a halt, raised his forepaw, and muttered one of his wicked spells. At once there was a sharp report, a cracking and crushing and grinding of ice, and the walls of my prison, already holding me like a vice, got smaller, pressed hard in on me, squashing, squeezing.

He vanished, to let his treatment sink in. And then he reappeared, more distorted than ever, more horribly playful. First his twitching snout, then his head, peeping round the corner, to scare his victim. I tried not to see it. Then the rest of him, all got up. He strutted about on his hind legs, very tall, wrapped in a long sheepskin and topped with an absurd black trilby. He came horribly close, leering in at me. Icebound, I could neither close my eyes nor turn away, but somehow I managed to raise an ice-fog between me and that awful sight. But I couldn't avoid hearing what he said:

"He doesn't want to see his dear friend Mr. Nicholas, the kind Old Gentleman who offered him that marvellous Black Opal. Well, he made his choice. He fell for the plain Jewel. He fell into it, ha, ha! He got what he wanted. Is he enjoying its wonderful Stillness?

"Quite like his dear old Clear Land, isn't it? But there are a few little differences, which I hope he's noting carefully. For a start, he's so small down here (isn't he?), so imploded, so boxed in by my own special brand of Stillness, Clearness, and (when I leave him to it) Silence. Not too much like the other sort up there, that took him out of himself, that sent him whizzing off in all directions. My home from home's made of deep-frozen space, just like that crystal in the middle of his precious Deep Map. Oh it's a pretty map that, and it led him to just the right spot, didn't it? Ha, ha!"

And he got up and raised his paw again—and again that terrible pressure, that implosion of Youlysees. Yes, I was being shrunk all right, getting smaller and smaller. He was a great Sorcerer.

But the most awful thing about his mocking abuse was that it was true. I wasn't allowed the comfort of being a martyr in a great cause, of being in the right. He'd have been less cruel if he'd lied to me. No, listening to him was like listening to myself, to the voice of my final despair.

He left me again to relish that despair, and was away so long that I began to hope he'd talked himself out. But no. I was in for another ghastly comic turn. This time he appeared enveloped in a huge sack with two disgusting eyeholes. Inside, he was doing a wriggling-poking dance back and forth, sticking out those blunted limbs at me. I frosted up that ice window a little more.

"Surely he wants to see his old friend Constable Luke, the hard-working guardian of all Flatlanders? Did he straighten up one of those hunchbacks? Did he ever learn, much less undo, my marvellous spell that blinds the silly fools to anything above and beyond their silly little heads? No! Mission failed! He made no difference to the world. Nowhere did he unflat them, un-flatter them. How perfectly my flattery, flattery, flattery-all-the-time works, as I whisper in their ears that they're the tops, with nothing higher! *Sapiens! Sapiens, Sap!*

"Now *he's* flattened. I've got him down in the dumps, in my Youlysees dump. All along I've been down-grading him. Now he's down to bedrock, rock crystal. Crystallised Youlysees!"

And he stuck out a tentacle, growled the magic word, and the ice came in. Where would it end?

How I wished I didn't have to watch another act, but here it was coming on now, this enormous shaggy absurdity strutting stiffly up and down on his hind legs, with a row of medals clanking on his stuck-out chest, a peaked soldier's cap at a jaunty angle on his head, and those long quivering ears sticking out.

"Thought e'd lost me, did e, Private What's-it? Got away wif hit? But hi've got im in me Cooler, me loverly Glassouse. What'll I do wif him? Use im as a paperweight hin the Regimental Hoffice. A bee-in-hamber. But much too much bee in this Hamber. Let's shrink im."

And then the inevitable spell, the crackling, the squeeze. He'd so nearly finished me that I thought he'd leave it at that, and not risk losing his prisoner altogether. But no. He came back at once, topped this time with a white skull—great empty eye-sockets and grinning jaws, nodding and chattering at me just inches away—all distorted by those icy walls.

"Didn't I warn the dear laddie in the Garden that his scene was there in Humania, where he'd found his Singer, heard the Song, accomplished his mission, arrived? Everything he's been up to—down to—since he sneered at my warning, has been undoing his mission, losing track of his Song, mixing up his world, killing himself by inches—the death of a thousand cuts. The Lower Arky's just another name for Defeat and Confusion—and Death! Why even his treasured memories are dying. Already he's remembering his memories of the friends he's lost—and soon it'll be his memories of his memories!

"He's made the worst of both worlds, he has, this Fool from Paradise. Lost for ever his dull old Clear Country, the Land of Wide Awake—wide awake to nothing!—and lost for ever my warm and glorious Coloured Country. Why he isn't even wide awake anymore—except to terror. This is the END, the VERY END."

He was right again! This was total terror! No, I wasn't terrified of him any longer, and not even of Death, but of terror itself.

And then even that went. That chattering, grinning death's-head uttered the spell, and those ice walls closed in for the last time and actually met, leaving not a bubble to mark the prisoner's grave. There was a tremendous crack. And then, SILENCE.

Chapter 19: Release

Silence … Peace … The peace of having nothing left to lose. … The peace before the world began.

And, now, arriving in that Silence, the music of creation itself— very faint at first, as it had been in the Clear Land, at the very beginning of the story.

And then the measureless expanse, the windless wind, the lightless light, of that Land.

And there, looming large in that expanse, I saw at last, undistorted now by ice or tears or terror, that bristling sharp-pointed, panting muzzle, tongue lolling over long bared wolf-teeth, and those wide-staring eyeballs. I took it all in as carefully and coolly as if it had been a picture in a story book. I explored those once nightmare features as if I were mapping the geography of yet another country I'd discovered. As indeed I had. And the best thing of all is that I didn't feel that I, in turn, was being explored and made something of by those eyes. There really was nothing here for him to look at. Nothing at all.

And then, as I gazed for the very first time willing and directly into the face of my ancient Enemy, I saw an astounding thing. Those foam-flecked lips weren't leering at me any more, or curling in contempt. That was surely the beginning of a grin! And that grin— why it was practically a smile! And that left eye: yes, it was actually winking at me! And soon those eyes were creased with laughter at the same moment. We laughed and laughed and laughed till the tears came, and half-blinded me again. And Oh it was the funniest thing, to be doing this together after our hundred-years' war. It was the best joke in the world, though if you'd asked me what the joke was I couldn't have told you.

But he drew back:

"You're not free yet. Only half the battle's won. Besides facing your Enchanter, you have to learn his secret name."

And at this he got smaller and greyer, and started barking and frisking about and leaping up at me, like a dog reunited with his master. And I couldn't make it out. Was this another of his games? Was he still playing with me?

But the momentary panic passed. Something in me responded, and I knew:

"You're ARGUS! Ulysses' faithful hound welcoming him home to his kingdom at last, at the end of his long travels."

"Yes, yes. But I have another name."

He grew big and wolfish again, and broke into his old hunting gallop. Then he produced from nowhere a huntsman's horn, and blew on it as he ran round and round me in circles.

And this time the answer came to me at once:

"You're the HOUND OF HEAVEN! My relentless hunter, the only one who wouldn't let me rest anywhere, who gave me no peace, until I came home."

And he went on racing round and round me in circles which grew bigger and bigger; and every now and then he stopped and produced a magical leaf-shaped mirror, and showed me my reflection in it. And what I saw was first Youlysees as a boy of twelve, then my

Laughing Angel, my Ringed Angel, my Spiral Angel—and finally, nothing at all. And then he came closer and showed me Gnomania, Goblinka, Elfland, the New Clear land—all the countries I'd visited on my travels, pictured here on the vanes of the Deep Map: the Map I made in the Library in Humania, with all those books and charts and models to help me. And then he came right up to me, so close that there was nothing to see—no atoms, no particles, not even space—just empty nothing.

And I saw that those pictures weren't even *slices* of the Deep World. There was nothing to them. They were airy and ghostly, magical shows, no more get-at-able than a rainbow or a mirage; and certainly not platforms anyone could arrive at or land on. And I laughed at how I had mistaken each one of them in turn for a solid and real world—till I'd been forced to look into it and go into it—and lose it. And that old devil kept me on the run till I reached the Centre; the Stillness, the Clearness, the Silence of my Home! The Home that, in fact, I'd never left! Only this stood up to close inspection. Only this was exactly what it *looked like!*

Now all the while that Hound had been making circles around me, something wonderful had been happening to the whole scene. My long imprisonment had left me dazed and near-sighted, so that at first I'd been able to see only my friend and his antics, with for background the clear and boundless space of Home. But now that space was filling up—filling up with winking, misty flakes and flames and sparkles of fire, flashing emerald and lemon and scarlet and crimson and sky-blue. Yes, of course, that was what it was. O happiness! It was the

Black Opal itself. But this time no egg-sized stone held out there in the hand; but that treasure filling the whole world: a skyful of ever-changing lights, a radiant colour-dome with me at the centre of it. With me as none other than that dome itself. Myself as the Black Opal!

And there he was still, Hound and Jeweler, large against against that jeweled backcloth, saying:

"Argus is my homely name. The Hound of Heaven is my magical name. But I have a third name, my secret and singular name. Until you've discovered that third name, the battle isn't won."

I stared long and earnestly into that wolf face, looking for any clue to that very secret name. And found none. But then those features slowly began to explode. Those eyes were growing larger and wider apart; those long ears were lengthening out of the picture; that smile was broadening till there was nothing left but smile. And then just an outrushing of vague shapes, a scattering mist, clearing …

And again I laughed, and laughed. That Great Enchanter, my deadliest Enemy, was MYSELF!

Hadn't I suspected often, in that dungeon, that his taunting was really my own voice telling me something I didn't wish to know? About my vanishing as myself, and my re-appearance as everything else? And as the night fog of my imprisonment melted into that bright and morning air, I saw that great Opal, with all its flakes and flashes of colour, take on the shapes of whirling spirals, of twinkling stars, of my Laughing Angel's spinning companions, of grown-ups and children and elephants and chimps and a very special cat, and that whole Lower Arky of gnomes and goblins and elves and tickles …

Why of course, my Black Opal was nothing else than the great ninefold Youinverse itself, the scene of all my adventures. And now all mine, all its depths within me, in an instant. Not for travelling in and through, this opalescent world! No distance separated me from those nine improbable glowing lands. Was I stretching right up to those stars, or had they come down all the way to me, so that I could cup the Twins in my hand, and flick the Great Bear on the nose with my finger? It comes to the same thing. I'd got the beautiful jewel, by being the plain one. How different and distinct those two jewels, yet how bound up together, how inseparable!

And then I had another vision. I saw a small but upright man in a dark cloak, a poet with sharp features sombre and lined with suffering, a refugee in a foreign land, near to his death. Gazing steadily into the Deep World, he was saying:

"Within its Depths I see gathered together the scattered leaves of all the universe, bound by LOVE into one volume."

Yes, that was it! The answer to the terrible spell that turns upstanding folk into Flatlanders, the great Counter-spell is LOVE! It's like putting your arms around the round world—the deep, deep world—and giving it a great big hug!

And next to that poet, I saw a tall wise man, a great Deep Map maker, who was telling a young girl at his side that it's LOVE which makes the world go round; then adding, with a wink and a nod:

"Yes, Alicia, it's also all those creatures out there minding their own business. For love is their business."

Alicia laughed. There she was at the very end of my Youniverse adventure. At the very start, when first her song sounded so faintly in the Clear Land, I'd supposed it came from the Silence of that country, the Quiet of my Home. What else was there to make it, who else to hear it? But I was after a more solid Singer. At first I thought it was a heavenly Singer—a Spiral or a Star or a Planet—and then I was sure it was this human called Alicia. But I was wrong again. The Song came *through* her, not *from* her. In fact, I'd never tracked down that solid Singer. And no wonder: I'd been right the first time. The Singer *is* the Silence, the Silence that I am. The Silence that *is* the Singer, *is* the Hearer, *is* the Author, *is* the Meaning, of the Song.

Listen!

MANY VOICES, ONE SILENCE.

MISSION ACCOMPLISHED!

Chapter 20: How It Ended

So that was it. Youlysees had come to the end of his adventures.

For a long time—it could have been a very long time—there was just silence. And then at last I roused myself, shivering. The fire had died down to a heap of ash and the lamp had burned out. I turned to my visitor to apologise. There was just enough light to see that his chair was—*empty!*

I started up and called out to him, but no answer came. I searched the cottage, in vain. I rushed to the door. It was already dawn, but the half-light revealed no footprints leading away from my threshold.

I went back and opened the window shutters. Outside, untrodden snow, and more snow, up to the forest. And, inside, that dead fire and the dreary furniture of my eventless everyday life, all of it saying that the young Prince from the Country of Everlasting Clearness and his adventures had been no more than a dream, a flight of fancy with no meaning for the rest of my too-predictable days, a night-time fantasy dissolving in the reasonable light of dawn. Everything added up to that forlorn conclusion.

With a sinking heart I flopped into the nearest chair. It was the one he'd sat in—(the one I'd *imagined* him sitting in)—all that time in the cheerful firelight. A terrible disillusion, a sadness for my whole un-risking existence, came over me. But I pulled myself together. Care and calculation and common sense prevailed. There was nothing to laugh about or wonder at. Everything was back to square one, to normal. But what a dismal norm it was.

And then that sudden mirage! At first, anyway, that was what it had to be—a vision of that model of his, his Deep Map, his rainbow-petalled cosmic flower, his good ship a-sailing back to his kingdom of Ithica and Argus his faithful dog. Its colours were alive, its crystal alight. The whole thing looked so brave and bright, just like him. If this was a vision, tell me: what do real things look like?

But it was no vision. I put out a hand and touched it to make sure. The early morning sun, venturing above that saw-toothed line of distant pines, had spared its very first rays to light up his gift, this keepsake and reminder, this token to remember him by. No danger of forgetting him now! And Douglas agreed. Curled around the base of the Youniverse, on duty as its guardian dragon was his friend, blinking in the faint sunshine and purring happily.

Somewhat dazed, I went on staring at that miniature, delicate nine-petalled flower a world, so unlike the bleak world of everyday life.

But then the truth of it dawned. Happening to look up to that East-facing window of mine, I saw the great Youinverse itself blossoming in its morning glory. There it was on show, beautifully set out petal by petal, vane by vane, all the way from the last lonely star in the blueing sky, the half disc of the orange sun, that curled feather of a cloud and the mountain tops all sun-guilded, the dark forest, snow on snow right up to my window. And then these shiny worn boards, Douglas yawning, these outstretched hands and arms, and—yes!—the Clear Land itself, this empty Heart. This full Heart already gone out to embrace all that scene, right up to and beyond that fast-fading star.

How mistaken I'd been! Youlysees' story was no fairy-tale with pictures, or Humanian Night's Entertainment. O no, the unreal, make-believe world was that flat, dreary scene which, in my first despair at his going, I'd seemed to find all around me. But now, really looking out, and really looking around, and specially looking in, why everything was as he'd found it, magical!

And then my eye fell on his second keepsake. Alongside the model lay a scrap of paper with a scrawled message. It was another of his conundrums:

RIDDLE-ME-REE
I've taken off, I can't be found,
I leave no tracks, I make no sound.

I HAVEN'T gone, I'm still around!
WHO AM I?

Appendix

The Top-Secret Song

1.

Young Man: You're nothing but a spinning top,
    a whirly, swirly, wobbledy top,
    spinning in the wind.

Alicia: Spinning high, spinning low,
    ha ha ha–little does he know!
    I'm the STILLNESS that makes the world go:
    I spin it fast, I spin it slow.
    You don't believe me?

Young Man: No, no, no!

Alicia: Try spinning yourself then. Isn't it so?
    Fly away spinning top. Where did you go?

Choir: Many spinners, ONE STILLNESS. Shshshshsh! TOP SECRET!

2.

Young Man: You're nothing but a painted top,
    a coloury, facy, racy topknot,
    facing the wind.

Alicia: Chubby cheeks or wan and hollow,
    rosy-smooth or pale and sallow,
    young and bright or lined and mellow,
    black or white or brown or yellow,
    ha ha ha—little does he know!
    I'm the LIGHT in which faces glow,
    empty for the bright rainbow.
    You don't believe me?

Young Man: I tell you NO!

Alicia: Look, look at yourself then. Does anything show?
    Fly away coloured top! Where did you go?

Choir: Many lampshades, ONE LIGHT.
    Shshshshsh! TOP SECRET!

3.

Young Man: You're nothing but a humming top,
   a trebly, trillaby, trumpery top,
   whining in the wind.

Alicia: Humming high, humming low,
   ha ha ha–little does he know!
   I'm the SILENCE from which songs flow,
   the silent seed from which they grow.
   You don't believe me?

Young Man: I tell you NO!

Alicia: Try hearing yourself then. Are you high note or low?
   Fly away humming top. Off you go.

Choir: Many voices, ONE SILENCE.
   Shshshshsh! TOP SECRET!